CALABRIA:
Mountains and Valleys

A NOVEL INSPIRED BY TRUE EVENTS

CALABRIA:
Mountains and Valleys

RAFFAELE ZUCCARELLI

ReadersMagnet, LLC

Calabria: Mountains and Valleys
Copyright © 2018 by Raffaele Zuccarelli

Published in the United States of America
ISBN Paperback: 978-1-948864-08-4
ISBN Hardback: 978-1-948864-30-5
ISBN eBook: 978-1-948864-09-1

All rights reserved. No part of this publication may be reproduced, stored in a retrieval system or transmitted in any way by any means, electronic, mechanical, photocopy, recording or otherwise without the prior permission of the author except as provided by USA copyright law.

No lines, parts and quotations were taken from other books or any previous publications. The opinions expressed by the author are not necessarily those of ReadersMagnet, LLC.

ReadersMagnet, LLC
10620 Treena Street, Suite 230 | San Diego, California, 92131 USA
1.619.354.2643 | www.readersmagnet.com

Book design copyright © 2018 by ReadersMagnet, LLC. All rights reserved.
Cover design by Ericka Walker
Interior design by Shemaryl Evans

*I owe my deep gratitude to Sylvia, who has been
my strength to pursue my dreams.
Whose love and thoughtfulness reverberates all throughout my whole
being. Through friendship and hard work, we made this book possible.*

I

For centuries, mankind has suffered toxic and deadly plague, endemics and harmful illnesses, and faced numerous cataclysms caused by natural events. And when it seems like these problems were not enough, man has created a way to fill in the gap with his own sinfulness, iniquity, unlawful act, felony, annihilation, and other shameful acts all throughout history.

Wicked people from different ages have caused suffering to an entire society.

Then there are events of self-serving violence for the purpose of jealousy and conceit which have adverse effect to his productivity, the peacefulness of his family, and the calmness at work. Even a family member can sometimes be the persecutor and cause tyranny to his own household. These events that were not told in history books are still spread through novels and short stories.

No one is immune to these loathsome events. It can happen to anyone, anywhere, regardless of the economic conditions. No one is excused to these detestable situations, no matter what your social rank is.

What is worse is that reacting to these situations is sometimes hard because of someone's inability to fight for himself. Fear and indifference also play a big role in hindering someone to react.

This saga narrates how a family wrestles against the abuses of an egotistic aristocrat. Its message extends to all pomposity, tormentor and sadism, and to the hallowed struggle adverse to those bullies who exploit their social position, abuse power, misuse women, and extort others.

When a cruel and oppressive ruler's arrogance and violence removes someone's power to act, speak, or think as one wants without hindrance or restraint and conditions, their lives to exasperation causes anger and hatred and a strong craving for human revenge.

According to the book of Deuteronomy in the Old Testament, "Vengeance is Mine", it is also written on the same book that "if a man hates his neighbour, assaults him, and beats him, the elders will deliver him into the hands of the avenger to be put to death."

Although revenge isn't one of the seven deadly sins, it may have the same gravity as the other seven; it may even be related to wrath.

Man, human as he is, can never carry the overwhelming burden forever.

II

The Great Sila, Calabria.

A PLACE WHERE THE AFOREMENTIONED abnormalities have yet to contaminate prides, its extensive flat land dips into valleys and plains with its thick forest vegetation.

Beach, chestnut, oaks, and trees of different variations provide a particular wood used by the ancient Romans to build the shells of ships.

The area looks like a huge crater formed by volcanic mountains, peaks arranged along the circumference, one next to the other.

Snowfall covers the plateau on winter season and clear blue skies on summer. Cold and clear streams can be seen on this steep and rugged terrain, their pathways interrupted by waterfalls. Deep caves have been carved due to erosion over time used by refugees or bandits who, for years, have terrorized unsuspecting travellers.

Wild boars and wolves are the dwellers of this magnificent area. Hawks called *adorno* also overflew this area, looking for prey for supper.

Artificial lakes occupy a rather large portion of the territory. The prominent and hilly land is rich with olive groves, vineyards, and citrus orchards.

The bleating of the flocks of sheep can be heard breaking the magical silence of the land, bellowing of cows, and the stamping and neighing of the horses.

Greeks colonized the territory during the ancient times. It was later inhabited by the greater population of the Bruzio, then conquered by the Romans, and dominated by the Byzantines, who were succeeded by the Arabs, the Normans, the Angevins, the Aragonese, the Spanish and Bourbons, and finally by the Italian Kingdom.

1927

This region, as with all of Southern Italy, rages with illness, destitution, ignorance, hefty economic deprivation and episodes of rampage as well as rampant act of banditing such as plague that the South inherited from the past centuries and is yet to heal. The brigands have often disguised their crimes by participating in patriotic uprisings, encouraging political movements, inciting riots, and riding social unrest against rulers to such an extent that they are treated as heroes by the townspeople who are unaware of their lawlessness.

The nobles demand respect and compliance. They must be greeted should a commoner meet them. Respect was highly implemented to the point of kissing their hands. They bear the title of Don, short for dominus; a reminder of superiority and supreme power.

Despite the violence they committed, these barons or lords still appear in religious gatherings, showing a facade of purity and kindness.

A Town of the Slopes of Sila

The streets are deserted because of the summer heat. Only the rushing water from the fountains could be heard. Those fountains are witnesses of history, used to quench the thirst and wash clothes of generations. In recent years, they've been used to soak the gorse fibers which were used to make fabrics for clothes. This is where women gather to talk, sing, and gossip. This is also where couples come to meet undisturbed.

The church bell chimes eleven beats. The shadows of the baronial palace looms over the square. The stone building is well preserved. Though it dates from the carved portal that bears the emblem of the house in bas-relief, one enters a large patio area overlooked by balconies with long wrought iron railings and by stairways from which one accesses the rooms of the palace. In the back there is a garden protected by a pergola and a path leading down to the stables.

On the second floor, from the balcony with a marble balustrade, Frank Cassano, almost forty years old, arrogant baron, the owner of the lands so vast, while sipping his tea, stares curiously, as if it were the first time, at the wine cellar with an adjoining shop across the square, which is run by two brothers. Frank Cassano is tall, strongly built and agile. He is proud and arrogant, his clothes elegant, and has hats for every occasion. Like those who came before him, Frank Cassano also keeps an army of well-trained soldiers to carry out orders from the baron such as collecting tax.

Frank Cassano doesn't trust anyone that is why his treasures are fenced in by his armed guards.

The Feud

Medieval system has remained unchanged over the centuries and still remained strong. This system is imminent through the baronial palace and surrounding dwellings. It is well-maintained by the interest of those in charge and the isolation from the rest of the nation, keeping the townspeople ignorant and preventing contact from the outside world. The baron only leaves for business or when he needs time for himself, but goes no further than Naples or Salerno.

He also has connections with business people from some cities in the United States where some of his native Italian and American friends reside. He exports wine and flavored vinegars which mainly masks the illegal business, shady dealings that are mainly drug trafficking, smuggling and black market pharmaceuticals.

Frank Cassano is ruthless and self-serving, only satisfying his greed for money. He has a circle of highly-placed and influential acquaintances. He has built himself a web of protection that is why most people consider him impenetrable.

His brother, Baron Don Alfonso, also possesses an equal vast estate which extends to Aspromonte and to the North borders the land of Frank Cassano. Bad blood is obvious between the two barons. Frank Cassano cringes at the thought of their lands touching each other that is why there exists a borderland. The baron is hot, wiping his forehead with a handkerchief while he confides a reflection of Luca, a thirty-six-year old conceited *consigliore*. He looks older than his age due to his beard and gray mustache.

"Antonio and Michael, brothers inseparable. I've never bothered those two. I've never thought of them but not this time. I need new men."

Under the reed canopy, in front of the store, is Franco, a high-spirited two-year-old boy, with his young mother Laura and his father Antonio.

Leaning against the door frame is Michael, a vigorous and good looking young man, with his arms crossed.

"Home and work. They mind their own business and are respected." continues the Baron. "Antonio could be a better Mayor compared to that ignoramus, Luigi."

The Baron enters the living room followed by Luca, leaving behind a trail of bergamot cologne mixed with sweat. He then lights a Cuban cigar.

"Imagine Antonio armed to the teeth," continues the Baron. "It's like having at your disposal an armed tank."

"And perched up there, at Varco del Diavolo," adds Luca, supporting the idea, "in that manor that looks like a fort.

"Yeah, a fort too close to the border with the land of Ruggiero. That damned fool could recruit him, but instead I will use Michael against him to destroy him! Go pay them a visit…and take with you the Albanian; you never know."

III

ANTONIO AND MICHAEL ARE the epitome of being a Calabrian: generous, sincere, and passionate. They loved their job and the land where they first took their first breath. The land is their second mother. Their parents started a bottle shop where they serve wine and, after a few years, expanded the store and started selling general goods. The two continued the legacy left to them by their parents.

Antonio is about twenty-five years old. He is lean, yet strong, a serious person, moody, distrustful, and heedful. He seldom bothers other people's business and loves a peaceful life. He lives with his young family in the apartment above the shop. He only leaves the shop should there be a need for shopping because he prefers to take care of it himself rather than letting his wife do the job.

Michael, the younger brother, only two years younger, is artful and scheming, taller and more good looking than his brother, Antonio. He is resolute and impetuous when making decisions. He occasionally helps his brother in the store and works at the manor, where he breeds horses. Having lived since childhood in contact with nature, he's had the opportunity for direct experience and has learned to listen more than speak, and to act at the right time. He's been married to Avellina months ago, skilled in making sweaters, blankets, and scarves from wool. They live in a cottage on the outskirts of the village, next to a citrus grove, together with her older sister, Antoinette, and together with her husband Mario and her daughter Carmela: a baby girl who has just had her second birthday.

Sitting at a table inside the store, Luca smokes his pipe while he speaks with Antonio over a glass of red wine. Leaning on the counter, the Albanian keeps an eye on them through the mirror.

Luca speaks in a low voice. "Often we misjudge certain people and when we get to know them; we find out how good men they are. Frank Cassano is cultured, loves literature, and knows the law and even Latin. His ancestors came into accord with the Bourbons, ensuring the obedience of the people, which goes on even today. He who is at the top doesn't want any problems, and Frank Cassano smoothes things out. In short, once can count on him, and he has political contacts and…" Luca pauses to chuckle, to hint that he prefers the criminal secret society, "No politicians. It is a privilege to be at his service and to have his protection!"

Antonio signaled Laura to take Franco away. "With all due respect, I believe I don't have the need for whatever the Baron can give me. I just mind my own business, period!"

But you saw it with your own eyes that nothing ever moves around here," insists Luca. "Here we don't have any type of control! Here there is no mayor, priest, or designee that counts. No, not one but the Baron. He commands and everyone obeys."

In the other room, Michael, intrigued, eavesdrops while he puts away some boxes. He opens the drawer to take out a gun and keeps watch from the curtain that separates the two rooms. Antonio, unnoticed, sees him and with a nod of his head tells him to go away.

"Whatever decision you will come up with", Luca concludes bitterly. "He awaits you at the palace to entitle you. To keep him waiting can be dangerous."

"A glass of wine." A customer orders.

Antonio goes behind the counter to serve the customer and fills up a glass of wine and hands to the customer and fills up another glass and hands to the Albanian, who has a grin on his face. Antonio puts out the pipe and keeps it in the pocket of his jacket.

Michael comes from behind the curtain and, taking advantage of the Albanian lifting his head to drink, whispers to Luca, "Can we have a talk?"

Luca, a little annoyed, obeyed.

Michael forcefully grabs him by the arm, he picks him up and nails him on the wall with one hand, while with the other he thrusts the gun under his chin. "What do you want from us?" asks Michael harshly with a hoarse and threatening voice. "Stay away from us! I do not argue things, I shoot!"

Luca trembles but kicks him and, moving, loudly knocks over some flasks and bottles on the shelves. An empty bottle falls down; it does not break, it slips under the curtain and slowly rolls until it's blocked by the Albanian's boot.

Antonio sweats because the man picks up the bottle and goes into the other room, draws back the curtain, and meets Luca, who on his way out, is fixing his tie. "I went to the toilet. Let's go!" Michael, behind him, takes the bottle and thanks him.

Luca furiously leaves the shop followed by the Albanian, who turns around to look at the brothers. Antonio and Michael look at each other, satisfied but suddenly worried.

The Varco del Diavolo

Few days later, Michael has to travel to the manor because he has to tend the horses. He is worried for having left Antonio all by himself to take care of the family and the store because he expects a reaction from the Baron. Although he knows of the violence the villagers are getting from the Baron, he never expected such to befall on his family. The cruel Baron runs all over the territory but Michael has never seen the Baron visit that part of the mountain. He just could not find an explanation.

Up in the mountain is the best and strategic way of dominating and controlling the entire valley. The air currents are compressed and channelled into a gorge in the valley where a cold, crystal stream runs and chilling people to the point that in mid-summer you feel the cold making credible the popular saying, "August, the start of winter."

A well-shod horse is needed should you ascend to that part of the valley. Once you get there, you will most likely feel lost or in a middle of a labyrinth with no exit. The horse must be trained to climb and descend each just as dangerous, to avoid the risk of breaking their legs, their skidding hooves making the rocks splash noisily as they try not to get stuck in the cracks or between the rocky spurs. The rider helps the horse, and the animal does the same, because progress is slow with nifty and nimble hops. Climbing by foot is also very strenuous, and, regarding orientation and knowledge of the routes, the same rules apply. This is probably the reason why no one dares to venture up there.

IV

It's the afternoon of a clear day. Gina, a slender girl, respectful and very eager, has offered to help Laura in cleaning and babysitting Franco. She is the only one who can make Franco eat without any hassle. She tells him her own stories and even makes voices for each character. She comes from a very poor family, having hardly anything to eat. She only asks for a little amount of money in exchange for her service. The family, out of kindness, offers her breakfast and lunch. They even let her bring some food for dinner when she goes home.

Down the trail, Gina pushes the stroller in which Franco is playing with his small horse toy. At the end of the trail, hidden by the lush vegetation, Luca and two stablemen peer maliciously with whips in their hands.

Luca lifts the latch of the abandoned entrance of the stockyard and, aided by his two accomplices, pushes the workhorses out with the cracking of their whips, their whistles and cries. The horses charge towards trail. Gina, scared, flattens herself against the blackberry hedges, scratching herself in several places, and leaves Franco on the trail, at the mercy of the rushing herd.

The raging horses collide with the stroller and overturn it while others that follow jump over it. They only slow down when they reach the clearing, and spread out.

With fear in Gina's eyes, she continues to scream and cry, while Luca, having completed the Baron's orders, laughs at the sight. Gina rushes to Franco, finding that he is not breathing and shows no sign of life.

Antonio and Laura immediately bring their child to the nearest hospital for emergency treatment.

Desperate and fearful, the couple waits in the hallway for the outcome of the examination the doctors are performing in the emergency room. Hours go by slowly, agonizing the couple as every minute passes by. Finally, the doctors come out of the emergency room and announce that Franco is in a state of coma. The prognosis is reserved, and he is to be kept under strict observation. Furthermore, there is the risk of tetanus infection because the terrain where the incident occurred is frequented by animals; horses in particular. Franco is transferred to the paediatric floor, where the parents enter to see him, though just for a few minutes.

Antonio and Laura hug each other, devastated and afraid. Laura cries at the sight of the inert and lifeless child. The night feels like the longest night in their lives. They ask permission to stay for the night.

After two days of exhausted waiting, the doctor monitors Franco. They administered medication, but the prognosis is still guarded, so they continue to wait. The parents are tired and emotionally and physically drained, as they haven't slept for many hours, yet they can't get themselves to leave their child.

On the third day, Antonio and Laura doze off on a white metal bench in the hallway. Despite the order of the Chief Doctor, Michael, together with Mario and Carmela, sneaks into the child's room. Carmela looks about; she is fearful, bewildered, and distressed by the environment. Antonio and Laura join them. They approach the bed. Carmela cannot reach to see her tiptoes, Michael lifts her.

"Franco," whispers the girl, while she tries to reach for Franco's face and caresses it.

With a shudder, Franco's arm moves a bit, and his eyes open slowly, confused and disoriented. He recognizes the familiar face.

With such excitement, the parents hug each other and joy fills the room.

"Mina," Franco manages to say in a faint whisper, almost incomprehensible.

Little do those two young souls know that an invisible bond between them is born, a magic thread that will stay with them forever.

Franco is discharged from the hospital, perfectly cured. "The episode will leave no trace." the Chief Doctor assures. During the convalescence period, the parents treat the child with extreme and exaggerated care. They fear that any strenuous activity may bring about complications even after many days.

Antonio, despite the seriousness of the fact, is not afraid. He stands strong in his position. The Baron, however, pulled the trigger first and already gave the first shot. Antonio and Michael are expecting another attack at any moment. They stand watchful and vigilant during the night. Even when they sleep. They stay awake, keeping their eyes and ears open for any noise out of the ordinary.

Strangely, nothing happens. It seems like the Baron is already satisfied with the attempt on taking Franco's life. In the previous years, the Baron never stood in their way; in the end, just provoked them and never summoned them.

A truce seems too good to be true. The brothers stay vigilant. They think this may be a silent tactic. A disturbing calm that frays the nerves.

V

A Year and a Half Later

IT IS NIGHT TIME in Santo Stefano when Avellina sets the table with a festive embroidered tablecloth, with the help of Aunt Lucia, who is celebrating Christmas with them. The aroma of fried *cullurielli* permeates the house. The whole family is about to gather around the dining table.

Michael hugs his wife. "I wonder what Antoinette prepared for dinner!" he says wittily. "She is bestowed with talent in cooking. Had I met her before you, I would have married her, of course with Mario's permission!"

Mario laughs and sits at the table with Carmela on his lap.

Michael leads the prayer before they eat. "We thank you, Lord, for the provisions and the bread that is on our table—"

"And for the pasta with olives that I like so much," interrupts Carmela. "Right, Dad?"

Mario strokes her hair, but her mother tells her to be quiet.

Just as they are about to start digging in, a knock comes from the door and Mario hurriedly opens it. Standing in front of him is a man with his face half-covered by a wide-brimmed hat. He has a cigarette in his hand. It is the Albanian. He kicks the door forcefully, pushing Mario backward.

Two armed thugs open fire on the furniture and the helpless ones present. Antoinette is killed and Aunt Lucia is struck down by a fear-induced heart attack.

Michael turns the table over to cover himself but a vase falls on his head. Carmela stumbles in the darkness of the adjacent room and with eyes wide enough to see the killer shooting Avellina. The Albanian finishes her father, Mario. After the terrible noise comes a deadly silence.

The merciless killers guzzle down wine from the bottles and from the kitchen take pieces of cooked meat with their hands.

Michael, still unconscious, with his face on the ground, slowly recovers but does not move. The Albanian, upon seeing this, thinks Michael is dead. Satisfied, they left and disappears into the night.

Michael is in shock. Carmela comes out from the comfort of the darkness of the corner, still covering her ears with her hands, throws herself to the arms of the man she thinks of as an uncle. She has lost everyone. He is all she has. Michael covers her eyes to spare her the details of the slaughter. He then plays the *malarruni*, the Jew's harp.

During the night, Michael doesn't sleep. He meditates and tries to find a solution without telling his brother. It is not wise to act immediately without thinking of a good plan. The family is so exposed to harm, so he decides to submit to the Baron and accept his protection. Only by being closest one to him can Michael find the appropriate opportunity to eliminate him for good.

The day after, he presents himself at the baronial palace. The Baron, diffident, studies him with suspicion, but since the "armed tank" can be useful to him for his criminal projects, he hires him.

In the study of Frank Cassano, in the presence of Luca, who acts as a witness, a loyalist with a sharp knife makes a small cut in the arms of Michael and the Baron. On the table, on top of a black tablecloth, is a missal and next to it a lighted candle.

A blood oath.

The baron wants to end the ritual quickly. The only thing that matters to him is to have Michael and to have bound him with a solemn promise.

"I pledge obedience!" Michael promises while drops of blood flow from both forearms.

They touch, and the blood mixes. "I pledge allegiance!" The rite continues.

"I pledge secrecy and silence!" says Michael as the two shake hands.

"Welcome among us," concludes the Baron. The hurried oath is finished.

Luca leaves for a few seconds and returns with governess Francesca, who leads Carmela by the hand.

Michael, realizing the situation, reacts violently and shouts, "Not this!"

"Obedience!" screams the Baron, angrily pointing his finger to the ceiling. Have you already forgotten?"

"But this girl has nothing to do with this!"

"I've always wanted to adopt a little niece," the Baron responds casually. "She will lack nothing. Francesca will look after her. She will study, learn music, play chess, and ride horseback. I am sure that by keeping her, you will remain calm and not come up with any strange ideas."

Michael's hand tightens into a fist, his face sweaty, his eyes closed, his lips pursed. The arrogant Baron grabs Carmela's little hands and pulls her behind him.

"But I don't want to! Zione!" screams the girl.

So Michael joins the men that make up the Baron's hands. Frank Cassano is not completely satisfied.

"That Antonio is unshakeable, but he is not a problem for now. I will leave him alone."

The Baron then lights a Cuban cigar from the box. "Damn, it's the last one. Bring me more from America!"

"Anyway, it seems that the Albanian's method is a lot more effective than yours, or have you already forgotten?"

Luca, embarrassed, does not reply.

With a slight bow, the consigliore takes leave.

The bullying continues over the years. Terrorizing the neighbouring areas. No one dares oppose him for the fear of being a victim. Antonio is no longer receiving threats from the Baron while Michael is being held in check by the fact that the man has taken Carmela for himself.

VI

1934 Ranch of Saint Domenico

The farmers are placing the crop bales in the barn, the groomers are taking the horses to the covered stockyard. The Albanian loads a sack of grain into the truck. Shouts and calls can be heard together with the rumbling of agricultural machinery.

Luca fans himself with his hat, drinks water with anise, and supervises, directing everyone.

At a distance, the singing of "Calabrisella Mia" in unison can be heard.

The Baron arrives in his carriage. He is smoking a cigar while observing and absently stroking the Neapolitan mastiff beside him.

Sante, a farmer, shouts in alarm, "Don Alfonso's picciotti on two cars!"

The Baron jumps to his feet in outrage while Michael draws near on horseback. "In broad daylight, not a wise decision!" They run into a hill where they can see the whole valley.

Around the bend, a Balilla and an Ardita ascend at full speed amidst a cloud of dust.

"He still cannot accept that I am the capo of the 'ndrina and he owes me respect!" The Baron says angrily. "This will be their last mission."

Along with eight men, the Albanian joins them on the hill, as does Luca with a horse for the Baron. They quickly go the warehouse where weapons are kept and distribute them. Then the armed men leave on horseback and arrive at the hill overlooking the village.

Looking through binoculars at the almost deserted square, the Baron sees some old ladies knitting in front of the doors of their houses, a man selling mostaccioli with his cart parked in front of the school, and two old men smoking under the shade of a small tree.

With clear gestures, the Baron assigns strategic points to the men, who one by one take their places. Then, with Michael, Luca, and the Albanian take their positions on a pergola-covered terrace.

Michael, with a liquorice stick in the corner of his mouth, looks nervously at the clock on the bell tower, which almost marks twelve.

"The children will soon be dismissed from their classes!" he comments worriedly.

The cars reach the first houses, and the frightened villagers barricade their doors and windows. The people in cars honk their horn, throw firecrackers, and blow loud whistles, covered by the chiming of the bells as the clock strikes twelve.

Antonio is out of town buying wood supplies while Laura barricaded inside the store, cannot go pick up Franco from school.

The school gates spread wide open, and throngs of school children come out with their papers and lunch baskets in hand, followed by teachers, spreading out loudly on the square and storming the cart of sweets. Franco and Carmela run joyfully, holding hands.

The cars break into the square, making carrousels, throwing firecrackers and firing into the air, creating panic among the children and teachers, who scatter to find shelter.

The Baron gives the signal and everyone starts shooting.

"Albanian, shoot at the tires!"

The Albanian follows the order and hits two tires, The Balilla crashes. "Got them right in the middle! Now they're screwed!" boasts the Albanian.

"Always infallible!" the Baron comments. "You, Luca, learn from this!"

Luca, green with envy, suffers in silence. The Albanian looks at him smugly.

The hit car ends its wild rampage, crashing against the wall and bursting into flames. The thugs emerge, disoriented, and are easy targets, falling one after the other.

"It is like we are shooting pigeons!" snickers the Albanian, shooting the tires of the second car.

"Be careful not to hit the children." shouts Michael.

The Ardita keeps running with its punctured tires, the rims sparking as it skids wildly, crashing near the terrace from which the Baron and his men are shooting.

The thugs come out shooting. The first one is hit by the Baron while the other two manage to get to the terrace. Michael guns one down, and the other, as he is about to shoot, is hit by Luca, who throws the knife with the carved wooden handle, hitting him in the chest.

"Great throw! Albanian, take note!" chuckles the Baron.

The Albanian is annoyed and scratches his head.

Frank Cassano approaches Michael and whispers, "With this system, each one of them gives to the max, and hating each other, they will not ally against me. The Romans called it *divide et impera*. You don't know Latin, but I see you understood."

Michael has a mischievous smile; by speaking ill of the two men, the Baron is using the same tactic with him. The evil Baron continues, "You, on the other hand, are a mystery, always quiet. You should hate me. Instead, these past years, you have shown me loyalty and fidelity. The truth is that, if you had wanted to take revenge, you would have done it already. No man is able to hold his anger for so long."

Michael knows that he wouldn't have been able to take revenge because the Baron is always armed and protected by bodyguards. Wisely, he has waited.

The last thug escapes, slipping into a ravine in the midst of a cloud of dust. Michael takes aim at him. The Baron, knowing that Michael will not miss the target, pushes the gun with his hand, causing him to misfire.

"Let him go. Let him tell my brother about the extermination!" He tells Michael.

Michael and Luca reach the dust-filled square, engulfed by the smoke from the firecrackers and the pungent smell of the burning car.

Carmela and Franco come out from their hiding place, terrified. In front of the entrance of the school are two students and a teacher, lying on the pavement.

Laura arrives and hugs the two children, sobbing. The other children, astonished and shocked, come out of their hiding places and slowly advance towards those killed.

The Baron, angry, now at the foot of the terrace, turns to the Albanian, "Who was in charge of the valley?"

At the moment, two guards arrive, sweating and panting. "We were on guard, but those cars passed at lightning speed!"

"And you allow them entrance to my house?"

He signals the Albanian, who immediately takes the gun and shoot the two guards. Although at a distance, the sound of the gunfire still attracts those on the square; all at once, the people still shocked about what happened, immediately look around to see where the sound came from. They see the Baron and the Albanian standing in front of the two corpses.

The mayor soberly approaches the crowd, looking at the present, tells them, "Whoever saw anything and wants to report can do so. You will now come down to the station to confirm it."

Franco is about to say something, but Carmela, still holding his hand, tugs at him and stops him.

Franco looks down.

Michael wants to get close to them, but the crowd prevents him.

The Baron approaches with an evil smile, arms folded. The crowd disperses and the officer, upon seeing the Baron, dismisses the case, as usual.

Farmhouse Quintilio

Don Alfonso, Frank Cassano's older brother, has a different character. His people respect him without him resorting to extreme violence, and he finds contentment when farmers and townspeople who work for him are able to maintain a certain level of welfare. As a youth, he studied at the seminary of Caserta but later abandoned his studies, preferring a secular life.

His wife died of infection, years after their marriage. Following his mother's death, his son chose to move to America where he has a ranch, using Don Alfonso's financial help and connection.

The killer spared by the Baron relates the failure of the mission to Don Alfonso.

"Next time, we will use more men." The Baron says. "By now, he must understand that we can attack any time. He should not keep too tight a grip; the townspeople might start a revolt that spreads like wildfire.

"We must maintain order and control the territory," Rocco, the Baron's consigliore adds as he approaches with his monocle to better examine the map, "but also provide jobs and organize festivities to keep everyone happy."

"He doesn't do any of this!" Don Alfonso asserted. "He is power-hungry and avaricious; he has taken over the territory, approaching the land of many farmers and causing their resentment."

The seized lands deprive many families of sustenance, reducing them to a state of extreme poverty and need. Don Alfonso disapproves and condemns this behaviour, provoking the anger and the death threats of his brother.

VII

1941

With the exception of having ordered the construction of a monument in honour of the fallen soldiers of World War I in the main square of the village, dedicated with a solemn memorial service, the Fascist government has never taken care of the town's residents, has ignored their existence, and has ignored their poor economic conditions.

But now, because the country is at war and men are needed for the Eastern Front, the state remembers them and takes them into account.

As a matter of fact, Antonio is called to arms and enlisted in a battalion of the Italian Expeditionary Corps in Russia.

Only one of the brothers will leave because both are "war orphans" since their hero father was killed in the line of duty in the previous world war.

Antonio entrusts his wife and son to Michael, who agrees to find the boy a job. The wine bar and bottle shop cannot be managed without Antonio, so he is forced to close both stores.

Michael goes to visit Laura, who is confused and worried about her husband's departure and the uncertain future that awaits her.

"Now that both stores are closed, Franco should look for a job. There might be a possibility on the Baron's ranch." Michael tells Laura.

VIII

Ranch of Saint Domenico

Franco is a slender and robust young man; he is beginning to care about his looks, to choose the way he combs his hair, to make his own decisions and to break away from his mother.

He tackles his new job with vigor and diligence. He likes to stay athletic and, to keep in training; he lifts buckets filled with water, climbs a telegraph pole, and dives from risky heights into heaps of hay in the barn.

Franco likes to read but must make do with the few books piled in Antonio's cellar, and to find a romance novel is a serious undertaking. Once in a while, he finds the courage to ask the old elementary school teacher who, satisfied with his request, gives him as a present a couple of books of adventures of Salgari.

In the stench of the stable, Franco, after he has replenished the manger with fodder, gathers hay for his bedding. Carmela comes in at a gallop on a bay. The young rider has a nice gait and looks arrogant in her splendour.

Franco hastens to meet her, helps her to dismount the horse, and together they take the horse to the manger. Making sure that no one sees them, they hug and kiss on the cheek. The young woman, her face flushed, stiffens for a few seconds and pushes him away.

"I had to jump through hoops to come work here, but you always avoid me, Baroness!"

"Leave me alone. I'm nervous," replies Carmela curtly, easing the tension.

Nicola is spying on them. He is consumed with jealousy and, when Franco tries to hug her again, he surprises them. "You are here to work, not to hug the girls, stable boy!" taunts Nicola with the arrogance of the master slave.

Nicola approaches them and pushes Franco away from the young woman, standing between them.

With the impetuosity of youth, the two adversaries clash and end up between the legs of the horses, who in turn become nervous and begin neighing and pawing the ground.

Carmela's gaze is frozen. She does not even tell them to stop but, rather, follows the fight with a sort of pleasure mixed with curiosity.

There is punching, tripping, kicking, throwing of objects, and screaming. Franco manages to pin the insolent Nicola, his back to the ground in dung.

"Stay in the shit, and don't try that again!"

Carmela, feeling an unconscious perverse pleasure in the violence, claps her hands enthusiastically.

Joining in the applause are the stable boys, who came in when they heard the noise and who happen to despise the losing party. Nicola gets up dirty, swollen with rage, and ashamed.

"Move that truck immediately," Nicola orders Franco. "I have to take out the tractor!"

Franco ignores the request, but Gervaso, the stable boy, generously offers to do it. "I'll take care of it!"

"Take care of yourself, I asked him!" Nicola orders him maliciously.

Gervaso, with a quick jump, is already at the wheel. He starts the motor. There is a powerful explosion.

The truck flies ten meters into the air then crashes noisily to the ground and explodes.

"God! That was for me!" whispers Franco.

Carmela, stunned and scared, presses him to her chest.

Nicola pretends to be surprised. "The gas tank had a hole; it was going to happen sooner or later!"

The Baron arrives, infuriated with Nicola, who, to alleviate his guilt, reports that Franco is courting Carmela and that he saw them hugging each other. The Baron looks sternly at the girl. "Go back to the palace; we'll settle this matter later! And you all go away! Go back to work!"

The Baron catches up with Carmela in her room and, enraged with all that Nicola has reported, furiously overturns drawers, opens closet doors, and takes out clothes, throwing them wildly onto the bed. He humiliates the girl, rubbing in her face all the luxury in which she has lived, and threatens that he will throw her out of the palace and shut her in a boarding school run by nuns in Naples if she doesn't end the relationship with Franco.

Coast of the Volpe

Michael shoots the rifle and hits the bottle he has placed on the rocks as a target. He gives the rifle to Franco and teaches him how to hold it.

"You have to hold it tight as if it were your woman because it can save your life. Like this, on the shoulder… Now seek the target, hold your breath, and shoot!"

Franco tries several times before he hits the first bottle.

Michael takes a stick, cleans it with his knife, and cuts it into pieces of the same size, which he places on the ground in a certain order, to simulate a pack of wolves.

"In a pack, there can be six or seven wolves that respect a hierarchy. The dominant one is at the head, and the others follow him. If you flee, they devour you; you have to remain still and wait.

The top dog growls and shows its sharp teeth and starts barking. It attacks you from the front, and to save yourself you have to give a mortal blow. Without the leader, the others stop and scatter, and when you yell to drive them away, they disperse. You are forced to kill the leader to save your life."

Michael shows Franco how to use a heavy axe. He hits the sides of a solid wooden pole several times. Then he takes a hay puppet, the kind that is burned in bonfires in village festivals and, after hitting it several times, throws the axe through the air and decapitates it.

Seeing the headless puppet fall apart, lose its straw and collapse, oddly enough, amuses them, and like two children they burst into loud laughter.

IX

Someone knocks violently at the door of the cottage. Michael opens the door and three thugs barge in, overturning chairs and furniture.

Frank Cassano, scowling, comes in behind them with his hands clasped behind his back.

"Marie, my undercover spy in Reggio, was caught in a raid!" the Baron shouts. "Do you know what the asshole did? He hung himself in jail, taking with him to the tomb the name of the spy who allowed Alfonso to blow the perfume deal I had in America! They say that he was caught because of a bitch's despicable accusation! But there is more; the herd raided ten days ago must be routed through the Varco del Diavolo. Do you know anything about that, or is my brother paying you? "I haven't seen any herd passing," Michael replies.

"I don't believe you! You knew about Marie. Who did you tell?"

"I told no one."

"I tell you who you told: your woman!" retorts the Baron.

"No, she has nothing to do with anything!" replies Michael.

"I don't believe you! I want proof of your obedience, a powerful demonstration," shouts the Baron.

Michael is confused and cannot foresee the Baron's intentions.

"I ask you again for a woman, Rosa! It is she who accused Marie, and you must eliminate her! Breve et inreparabile ternpus, omnibus est vitae!"

Michael doesn't understand the meaning of the phrase. He is stuck, quivering with rage and cursing through his teeth. "Not Rosa! I can't do it!" he cries and shakes his head in despair.

Marie was a thief. Two years earlier, to save himself from an accusation of theft, he vilely had the loot discovered in the room of Rosa's brother, who was unjustly sent to prison.

Rosa had sworn she would make him pay.

Even in the midst of war, the patron saint is celebrated in order to respect tradition and invoke help. The Church dedicated to Saint Catherine of Alexandria is a Romanic styled, three-nave church with marble columns, embellished with paintings and sculptures such as a tabernacle made of wrought silver, and the obligatory statue of St. Francis of Paola, protector of the whole region.

St. Catherine lived during the fourth century, A.D., and the reality of her life is often confused with the popular legend. The young woman was summoned by the Roman governor to Alexandria in Egypt, where theologians appointed by the governor himself were ordered to persuade her to honor and offer sacrifices to the gods; but it was, in fact, the girl who converted the group of scholars to Christianity. Catherine and the philosophers, who had failed in their intent, were sentenced to death. The Saint is now the patron saint of theology students, young seamstresses (also known as the catherinette), and potters.

The patron feast is celebrated at the end of November, in the midst of fall. The morning of the feast day, a musical band formed by very few members, goes through the little streets of the village, followed by the children and some villagers.

At noon, after the liturgical rite at the church, the bells ring in celebration, and the procession starts in a pre-determined order. At the tail-end of the procession are the faithful, as well as some villagers who, according to tradition, dress in historical costumes.

Sacred chants, litanies and prayers accompany the statue of the saint—a crown on her head, dressed in royal robes, a palm and a book of knowledge in one of her hands, and in the other the sword and cogwheel with which she was killed—through the narrow streets of the village, the saint carried on the shoulders of the men of the Confraternity, among whom is Franco, wearing a white robe tied at the waist with a cord.

Laura is not able to follow the procession, so she waits in front of the house for it to pass through. Many women have tears in their eyes for their child, their husband, or a relative who has left for the war. Once in a while, an old lady may scream out invocations addressed to the saint. Such an invocation is soon answered by a grand choir of parishioners.

To pay homage to the saint in the procession, from the windows flower petals are thrown decorated with white embroidered linen sheets and blankets made of damask. Once the procession has completed the rounds of the village, having reached the square, it stops in front of the baronial palace in reflection, awaiting the first gunshot in honor of the saint.

Frank Cassano, with a stern attitude and arms folded, looks from the balcony at the crowded square. Luca stands behind him. Flora, accompanied by the governess, leans out the door just enough to catch sight of the people. The shots end and the bells begin ringing in celebration; the procession continues its march.

The venerated statue sways slightly during the transport back to the church, due to the unevenness of the road. Once the church is empty, Frank Cassano, alone, goes directly to the statue of the saint, lights a candle beneath it, and exits immediately.

While the ritual of the procession is being carried out, another ritual, a serious and deadly one, is about to take place. To be carried out is the execution of an order of death, issued by a cruel tyrant reminiscent of the Roman governor who sentenced Saint Catherine to death. The perfidious man is part of the cruel twists and turns of historical events.

Michael arrives at the house of the girl, who is by herself because her family is out working in the fields. He dismounts his horse, and Rosa, with the white dress for the festival worn under her cloak, runs toward him and hugs him. She knows that he has come to take her to the village.

The man is silent, sullen, and the girl hugs him worriedly; she doesn't understand. Michael, as he hugs her tightly, covertly pulls a knife from its sheath. A desperate look and he strikes. "Forgive me. Forgive me!"

The blade sinks into the abdomen of the unsuspecting and innocent young lady; she opens her eyes wide. A blood stain appears on the white dress that at first slowly, then quickly and inevitably, expands while the body slumps and slides to the ground between the shaky arms of the man.

Michael places the girl in a cart, very delicately as if he were afraid to hurt her, and takes her to the Baron's ranch where he holds a wake over her the entire night. He is unable to shed a tear, and this burns him inside. He would give anything to be able to scream, to rend, to vomit, but he can't. He is cold, alert, and rational. The malarruni sounds at dawn and the farm workers arrive, surprised to witness the deceased young woman. They make the sign of the cross in consternation and look at each other in solemn silence. The Baron on horseback in the distance hears the sounds but doesn't come near.

Franco meets up with his uncle at Varco del Diavolo and tries to comfort him. Michael is bewildered and does not yet realize he has committed a crime. The loss of Rosa has left him with an overwhelming emptiness; he will never forgive himself for having blindly obeyed the orders of the cruel and infamous Baron.

"I have sworn revenge and he will pay. He has taken too many lives. I had to give into his tyranny, but I have a plan, and a person who will help me," Michael told his nephew.

"But he has many men on his side; he is the head of a gang," cautions Franco.

"The head of a pack! And we will fight them as if they were wolves!" replies Michael.

The war spreads like wildfire, involving more and more nations, with more fronts being opened on land, sea and in the air. The toughest battles take place in Africa, with ever-changing outcomes.

On the vast Eastern front, repeated attacks from the Russians, and unfavourable climatic conditions, prevent or delay military successes for the Italian soldiers.

X

Laura hears no news from the front. She is ill during the sad and monotonous days that pass. She has constant anxiety attacks. At night, she is troubled by recurrent nightmares, and it seems that she suffers, from a distance, the same hardships and dreadful vicissitudes as Antonio.

She never leaves the house anymore and expects at any moment bad news regarding her husband.

Michael and Franco, armed with rifles, are going to hunt wild boars. Franco is about twenty feet in front of Michael. They venture into the forest, go through it, and come out into a snow-covered clearing.

From the top of the hill comes a disorderly pack of seven wolves, howling and running towards them. Hungry and panting, they freeze about ten meters from Franco.

Michael stops, stands still, and orders Franco, "Fire at the leader of the pack!"

Franco points the rifle but, because of the cold, the weapon is jammed; he tries again, but it still fails. He is stuck. Despite the cold, he is sweating. The cold air freezes his throat but his hands, that were numb in reaction, begin to warm up and he can move them well.

Michael cannot shoot the beast because Franco is covering the target.

"Use the axe!"

Franco drops the rifle, which quietly sinks into the snow, and pulls the weapon from its sheath.

The leader of the pack jumps and shows his teeth, growling, the other wolves frantically agitated. Franco is about to take a step back, but Michael, determined, stops him.

"Don't retreat!"

The wolf lowers its head and slowly starts to come near. Franco can see the vapor coming from the animal's humid nostrils; he feels the heavy breathing of the wolf, which is joined by the others'. They pant in a disharmonious chorus. The leader barks and continues to advance followed at a distance by the pack. It suddenly jumps to the side and begins approaching, ready to pounce.

Franco stares intently into the glassy eyes of the beast. He goes to attack and, before it jumps, hits the animal on the cranium, smashing the frontal bone. The animal gasps and collapses.

There is a pool of blood on the snow. There are resonating howls from the female and the rest of the agitated pack. In confusion, they run around and disband.

Franco lifts his hand threateningly with the blood-stained hatchet and runs toward them screaming, "Get!"

The wolves, without their leader, flee howling; they disperse into the forest.

"You did it!" shouts Michael.

Franco gives a deep sigh of relief. "Whew!"

XI

Antonio, a war veteran, walks home from the catastrophic Eastern front. He was sent home after suffering frostbite on one of his feet while stationed in Russia in below-zero temperatures. His foot is completely immobile. The man has been sorely tried in body and spirit.

Antonio has stared death in the eyes; he dreams of telling Laura all the terror he has endured, facts that would make anyone cringe. He has the need to share with his wife his ordeal so he can better endure the weight of his sad memories.

After repeated defeats on the battlefield, the human tide formed by demoralized and distraught soldiers heads out on the road that will take them home, an unknown destination at a dreadful distance.

The environment is endlessly white, a land surrounded by a white membrane of humidity and frost, without horizon, where the more you walk the more it gives you the impression that you have not taken one step, so much the same is the hellish landscape. And to think that one imagines hell as a hot and fiery place.

He can't speak because his lips and mouth are dried out and numb; his nose is encrusted with frozen mucus like a stalactite.

He must walk fast to avoid being strafed by planes that occasionally pass by. His baggage has the strictly necessary, almost nothing, as what he had taken along is either frozen, destroyed, or rendered unusable.

When finally he arrives home, as he recounts his tale, Antonio cannot shed even a tear. His cry is an internal one; the tears fall on the inside. His are stories that freeze your spirit just to hear them.

The wounded and the sick that couldn't make it were abandoned. Hunger haunted them and, despite all that snow and cold, he was always thirsty. There was no drinking water. The nights were sleepless because, if one slept or even stopped for a moment, he passed from sleep to the eternal rest beneath an icy sheet of snow.

Stubbled beard, frozen ears, filthy bodies; they were sent into the fray without proper winter attire, without proper weapons, with shoes and boots with pressed cardboard soles that swelled and burst, ripping open like hungry mouths.

A foot got frozen. He limped, he dragged it. Someone offered to help, to generously take him a few meters, then the other, more tired than he dropped him.

Finally, the rescuers, the Red Cross, arrived. It was a blessing to be sick and disabled.

The repatriation took place on very cold trains, long stretches on board open cargo cars until a crowded military transfer unit was reached.

He left behind many dead, wounded, or confused and scattered soldiers.

Upon arrival of the train, thousands of people assaulted him, grabbed him by the sleeve of his coat and pulled him. They held out pictures of their loved one, comrades not yet returned.

In the chaos, they asked, insist, demanded, to know if he had seen them, and when he could not provide news, they pushed him away and moved on to torment the next veteran.

The disabilities of these men notably reduced their ability to work; still, Antonio decides to open the tavern and the shop with the help of Laura and Franco. He will later be given a military cross and a pension.

The war has an evolution. The Allied troops land in Sicily, cross the Strait of Messina, and go up the peninsula. They travel through Calabria but don't stop; they go north.

After a few months, the fascist regime falls, but the war against the Nazis continues. In Italy, the Resistance against the Nazi fascism begins and will later bring the final victory, the Liberation.

XII

Ranch of Saint Domenico

The tenant farmers in line take turns laying the bags of grain on the big scale. It's the Albanian's turn, and he places the sack on the scale and, making sure Nicola doesn't see him, presses his foot on the platform, and the weight goes up.

"One hundred and ten kilos!" shouts Nicola, who notes the weight in the book.

Luca, leaning against a pillar, notices the Albanian's trick. "The retribution to Frank Cassano is due in full. Do you think he likes your miserable tricks?"

"What do you care?" the arrogant Albanian replies. "You too steal from him!"

"But you have no proof!"

Luca grabs the bag, puts it back on the scale, and shouts, "Eighty kilos! Write it down!"

"Christ! He was cheating by thirty kilos!" replies Nicola, appalled. He quickly corrects it in the book.

"Let's hear what Frank Cassano thinks of this," says Luca triumphantly. Turning to Nicola, he says, "And you, pay close attention when you work!"

In front of the farmers, stable boys, and guards, all gathered in the forecourt of the ranch, the Baron, frowning, arms folded, passes in front of the general staff of his gang. "I know there have been attempts to defraud me on weight…and this is a sin. They say that you should condemn the sin, not the sinner, but I think differently. I want to know the sinner, and to make him pay!

In fact, Luca has told me who the sinner is!"

Frank Cassano stands in front of the Albanian, stares at him menacingly, then goes straight to a nearby table, picks up a billhook, and feels the edge of the blade with his index finger. "You are a thief, and I have to chop off your right hand. I cannot let it pass, dura lex!"

The Albanian is terrified, but contemptuously he holds back his fear. The Baron gives a sign, and four brutes hold him down. Then, merciless, the Baron gives the billhook to an executioner. His index finger over the man's sweaty face, he says, "But I will give you a break because of your exceptional aim! You will only lose your left index finger. You'll still be able to shoot for me with the right!"

The men tie the arm of the Albanian to the wooden counter. The billhook is raised. Unforgiving, it strikes! There are agonized screams from the man, and disgust from all present.

The screams reach Carmela's room on the first floor of the farmhouse. She remains cold, impassive, staring into space. She remembers when the Albanian killed her father in cold blood. On Carmela's face there is an evil smile of satisfaction for the vengeance, and of admiration for the powerful Baron. She orders the horse saddled to return to the baronial palace.

The Second World War is over. Italy is a free, democratic, and independent nation.

Slowly, the country returns to social and political normalcy with the establishment of a provisional democratic government, in charge during the transitional phase before popular elections.

XIII

The war between Frank Cassano and his brother, after a brief respite, has resumed.

Don Alfonso has diverted the course of the river, and some of his brother's pastures are drought-stricken, endangering the survival of the herds. In fact, some of the cattle, the calves, in particular, are already dying.

Frank Cassano, provoked, orders his men to transfer the cattle to the pastures further north, with all the difficulties this operation entails, while he ponders revenge against his brother. He orders Michael to make an inspection of the land to learn what system was used to harness and divert the waters; he fears the same disaster will happen again in another part of that damned border, the thorn in his side.

On one of his escapades to Salerno, Frank Cassano meets Sofia, a gaudy, second-rate ballerina, much younger than he, after seeing her in a show at the Marechiaro Theater. It's love at first sight, and he decides to marry her without delay.

The marriage is celebrated on a sunny spring Sunday, in the presence of many guests. The newlyweds, in splendid garments, exit arm in arm from the church that is decorated with fragrant broom bouquets, Mendelssohn's nuptial march still playing in the background.

Sofia throws the bouquet and Carmela grabs it with a jump of joy. Handfuls of rice, confetti and rose petals, applause, and "Long live the bride and groom!" follow the newlyweds out of the church. After the wedding, there is a sumptuous wedding banquet with speeches and toasts.

The whole Village is celebrating. It is a day of truce in which the Villagers seem to have forgotten the injustices of the Baron and hope that his marriage will change him for the better.

In their hopefulness, they are merry and set up their modest tables with simple, authentic dishes, starting with different seasoned olives, from antipasti to beef, pasta a la fumu, mazza corde, broucculi 'fungati, and frittuli. The air is impregnated with the aroma of rosemary, garlic, and sautéed onions, while red rivers flow from the Pollino. And to conclude the meal, desserts include giurgiulena, pitta 'npigliata and the obligatory dried figs.

At sunset, a folk group in traditional costumes performs popular songs. The players of the arganettu, ciaramedda and Tamburello, take their places; it is the moment of the vidanedda, a dance that goes back to the culture of great Greece and awakens ancient rites and evokes symbolic figures.

The dance is a sort of tarantella, a choral and yet a couple's dance; a mutual dialogue, an exchange of love with sensual messages, as in the courtship ritual, in which the man exhibits his physical strength and is admired by the woman he loves. The people are arranged in a circle, the "rota" (wheel), and the maestro d'aballu (dance teacher) is at the center because he is the boss, the charismatic figure who leads the dance.

The teacher shouts the name of a man, pairs him up with a woman, and makes them dance. A few turns and twirls and saying, "Out the first!" the teacher tells the man to exit, with a "Thank you, ma'am," tells the woman to exit, and calls out another man or woman to dance. The new couple goes on until one of them is asked to exit, then is replaced by another dancer, and so on. Meanwhile, all those waiting around the circle clap their hands.

"Out the first!" The male dancer exits.

"Franco!" shouts the teacher and Franco enters to dance with the woman already in the centre of the circle.

"Thank you, ma'am!" The female dancer exits.

"Carmela!" shouts the teacher and this girl enters the circle to partner with Franco.

Carmela is very beautiful, now a woman. The Baron, a bit tipsy, goes to the front row when he hears Carmela's name and watches the young woman with lust, forgetting his wife, who tugs on him with jealousy.

Michael, trying to forget, has drunk a glass too many; he is dazed but notices the Baron's blatant attitude as his wife takes him away.

While Michael watches Carmela dance, his vision becomes blurred…and the girl takes the form of Avellina wearing the traditional costume. Gunshots echo in his head…and now he sees Antoinette dancing with the blood-stained white dress…swaying, Michael reaches the fountain and dips his head in the water. He sits down and rests his head against the wall.

Franco looks at Carmela…eyes as black as coffee, as black as coal, as black as squid ink.

> Eyes that laugh and shed a river of tears of pain and pleasure; that make you, too, laugh and shed a river of tears of pain and pleasure. Eyes that speak without uttering nonsensical words and touch without using unnecessary hands; eyes that call and shout; that incite and whisper. A gaze that comes from the depth of her being to enter the depth of your being. Shivers. A knot in the throat. Excitement. Desire. These are Carmela's eyes.

Carmela interprets the figure of the amphora. She moves with grace, she dances with her hands resting on her hips, to highlight the pelvic area, a symbol of woman's fertility, motherhood, the carrier of life. Franco claps his hands in the air then under his leg as he lifts it. He dances slowly at first, then faster and faster as he turns Carmela around. It is the siege of love from which the woman, spinning by herself and moving away, pretends to escape, but then gives in to because she desires to be courted and loved.

Carmela mischievously drops her muccaturu, a lace handkerchief, to show her acceptance of courtship. Inebriated and excited, they dance shoulder to shoulder then slowly sneak away. They run to the washing fountain, where they know no one will look for them that night.

When mad with love, any place is good. They lie down on a wooden bench, submerged under a pile of dried laundry stacked together. They laugh, then are quiet and serious. The enchantment of the silence is broken by the harmonious and crystalline sound of the water falling into the basin of the fountain.

Embracing, they give themselves completely to each other, enjoying their stupendous and a long night of love under the moonlight that filters through the great arches, and illuminated by the colorful and varied flashes of fireworks.

Again, Carmela suddenly stiffens and bursts out in a hysterical cry. Franco gently hugs her to reassure her.

The nation is heading toward an important decision that will institute either a monarchy or a republic by means of a historical referendum. But even during great changes, history teaches us that many times, nothing changes.

Groups of power and supremacy, much like the chameleon, are able to maintain their position, privilege, and prestige, regardless of popular choices, changes in regime, or institutional reforms. These are untouchable people, skilled manipulators, crafty politicians, opportunists, and social climbers. These people are "corks" that will never sink because they know how to get back into the circle. They cunningly know how to render themselves useful and appear indispensable; they are the propellers, people who know how to cleverly ignore the past. The Baron and his gang are among those people.

Despite the changes, there are subtle arrangements, treacherous exchanges, and favours, which is why some areas continue to be isolated and under the domination of the previous owners. A cone of shadow, a dark corner, such is the evil of every free and civil society, an evil that unfortunately exists. If there is an area of good, there is one of evil, whether absolute evil or just the absence of good.

XIV

Ranch of Saint Domenico

In the barn, where bales of hay are stacked, Franco, bare-chested and wearing a red hat, piles the hay with a hay fork.

Carmela arrives on the cabriolet. They hug and, while they kiss, the young woman startles and abruptly halts her embrace. Carmela loves Franco, but her fears make her reject Franco's acts of affection.

Her young life, at a certain point in time, was changed by the witnessing of violent acts which throttled and crushed her feelings and emotions. She is torn between love and violence. Her feelings of love are still alive but have been repressed; they are the same as that day when a gesture, an affectionate caress, coincided with the awakening of Franco from a coma.

The Baron's car pulls into the farmyard. He is accompanied by the glamorous Sofia, wearing an elegant, tight, pink cotton dress. Frank Cassano honks the horn several times and shouts, "Franco!" Carmela dives into the hay behind the bales, and Franco comes out. "At your service, Baron!"

Sofia is attracted to Franco for his good looks but cleverly conceals her desires.

"Go to the Fontanone and bring three horses for the guests arriving Sunday. Pick the best!"

"It will be done, your lordship!"

Carmela gets up cautiously and flees without being noticed, while Franco wipes the sweat from his forehead with his arm and goes back into the barn.

The Baron smiles at Sofia.

"Wait for me here while I check on a cow to see if her calf has been born.

Nicola arrives, panting. "Frank Cassano! Frank Cassano! I heard on the radio that the republic won! You told me to vote for a king. What will happen now?"

The Baron is not at all troubled; rather, as he strokes the mastiff lying on the back seat of the car, he shows the rough stable boy his defiant confidence.

"Here, absolutely nothing!" the Baron replies with a wry grin. "The governors come and go; they are men, and men always yield. The butts change, but the corrupt seats of power remain the same! At any rate, it is none of your business. Go take care of the bales of hay!"

Sofia, annoyed, contemplates and executes a daring plan. She enters the barn, pretends to stumble, and asks for help for a sprained ankle.

Franco rushes to rescue her. The seductive woman, sitting on the stool, takes his cap off, looks him in the eyes then stretches her leg, bares it, and offers it to him to massage it with the intention of ensnaring the young man.

Franco tries to contain his instinct but, excited by the forbidden fruit, he gives in to the provocation. He doesn't think about the risk he is taking. Perhaps, unconsciously, he wants to hit the Baron somewhere untouchable and sacred.

The woman wraps him between her sinuous arms, and Franco lets himself be sucked into the pleasure.

At that very moment, the Baron enters, worried and furious because the cow is having a difficult birth and may die. "What are you doing?" He yells like a madman.

Sofia keeps silent, and Franco, embarrassed, passes his hand through his hair. "I assure you, nothing happened!" Franco stammers.

The young man puts his cap back on, dashes out, jumps on the truck, and leaves at full speed.

The Baron looks scathingly at his unfaithful wife. "It is as he said? Nothing really happened?"

The woman defends herself, but the Baron doesn't believe her and slaps her.

"Whore! You have condemned him to death!" He growls in a low voice, to not be heard by others around.

Nicola, who saw Franco escape, comes rushing in. "What did he do? Why is he running away?"

The Baron points the gun at the woman's head then snaps and gives the gun to the stable boy.

"Chase him with the car, and kill him like a dirty dog!"

Sofia, her hair dishevelled, her dress wrinkled and her cheek reddened from the slap, exits the barn and passes like a bolt by Carmela, who can already picture what has happened. It confirms everything when she sees Nicola in the Baron's car, leaving in pursuit of Franco. Carmela wants to find Franco to warn him of the threat he is under and to clarify the situation in her own mind. She knows where he is hiding. She goes toward the cabriolet but figures that it will take too long, so she opts for a horse. She doesn't mount right away, remaining thoughtful a few seconds. Something is making her hesitate. She finally decides and jumps on the horse's back.

Beech Forest of Colle Gioioso

Franco, sweating, is leaning against the horses' corral. He rests his head on the fence. Carmela arrives, breathless on the sweat-drenched horse.

"Maybe I should have avoided this gallop. Let's hope for the best!" says Carmela.

"What do you mean?" asks Franco

"Nothing," she replies. But Carmela hits him with a violent slap, then, regretful covers his mouth with a kiss. "Traitor! And with a fourth-rate ballerina!"

"She provoked me, and I lost my head. That's all!"

"Be careful because the Baron has sent Nicola to make you pay!"

"Let's go to Zione at Varco del Diavolo," Franco suggests.

"No one will dare to go up there!"

"And the truck?" says Carmela, worried. Aberto, the stable boy, hears them and comes near. "I'll take it back, and tell them that I saw you run off across the beech forest."

Franco, out of gratitude, takes his cap and gives it to Aberto as a present.

"Take it. It's yours!"

"Thank you. I will say that you lost it while you ran." He puts the hat on his head and leaves.

Nicola has stopped the car right at a bend. With the Baron's binoculars, he scans the territory and spots the truck. Now he takes the precision rifle from the trunk, positions himself on top of the roof, and when the truck comes around the curve, recognizing Franco's cap, fires two shots that puncture a tire. The vehicle swerves, rolls into a ravine, and bursts into flames.

Varco Del Diavolo

Outdoors, sitting at a rustic table illuminated by an oil lamp, Franco and Carmela are having a snack.

Franco cuts a slice of bread, spreads on it the 'nduja, and offers it to Carmela; he prepares a second one for Michael who, worried and thoughtful refuses and takes an olive instead.

"You touched a nerve there: jealousy. He will give you no respite. To strike you will be his reason for living. He might even put a price on your head. You can't stay here. You have to leave. Go far, very far," Says Michael.

"What do you mean by very far?" asks Franco.

Michael spits the pit of the olive into his fist and responds assertively, "to New York, in America."

"In America? But I am—" Carmela anxiously intervenes but quickly stops herself.

"I will bring forward the plan I've had in mind for some time," continues Michael, "You will go to Uncle Salvatore, called Zio, and will give him a letter."

"But Zione, I don't even know where this city is, and I don't speak a word of American!" replies Franco, his ears red with emotion.

"Zio will teach you," retorts Michael firmly.

Carmela relieves the tension by sneering at the curious nickname. "Zio? What does it mean?"

"I'll tell you someday," Michael replies, "I'll let him know of your arrival. He is the owner of the restaurant Casa Mia. Aunt Agnella helps him run it. Tomorrow, I'll take you to Naples and there you will embark on the Mazzini. I'll speak with Antonio and your mother afterward. Let's go, Carmela. I'll take you back to the palace!"

Flora, afflicted and crying, hugs Franco; both must resign themselves to their inevitable fates.

Franco will embark on one of the few cargo ships that have resumed sailing the transatlantic routes.

Michael warns Franco that he must not write any letters, so as to not reveal his hiding place.

"Franco, I wanted to tell you—" Carmela tries again, a bit jittery.

"Nothing, nothing. Never mind."

Michael and Carmela leave on horseback.

Franco is anxious, pacing nervously back and forth for almost an hour. Then he makes up his mind and goes to saddle the horse in a hurry to make up for lost time.

The power and irrationality of love!

The guards go back and forth along the perimeter of the baronial palace.

Franco stands on the horse's saddle and climbs on the trellis. A supporting beam breaks and he falls, stuck, his feet hanging in the air. He manages to climb back up and reaches the balcony of Carmela's room. He enters with caution.

Carmela sleeps restlessly. Franco moves near her and gently wakes her by covering her mouth with his hand so she won't scream.

Carmela pushes his hand away. "You're insane! They have doubled the surveillance"

"I want to know what you wanted to tell me earlier," Franco replies.

Carmela hugs him, ecstatic. "You took such a risk for that? Here, I wanted to tell you that I…I'm pregnant!"

Franco bursts with joy. "This is fantastic! That's why you wanted to avoid the gallop to Colle Gioioso. How am I supposed to leave now?"

"You absolutely have to get to safety. This baby must not be born an orphan. We will wait for you!" Carmela reassures him.

Luca makes the rounds for inspection and finds Franco's horse tied to the tree; he touches it and feels it sweaty. Looking toward the palace, he sees Carmela's room illuminated. Then the light goes off. He motions to two armed guards, who take their places.

Franco climbs over the balcony, holds onto the rail, slides down the pergola, and finds the barrels of rifles pointing at him. Luca fires a shot into the air to give the alarm.

Carmela, worried, leans over the balcony, her view hampered by the foliage of the pergola. She can't quite understand what's happening from the shouts of the Baron, who, not quite awake, looks out the window to see Luca holding Franco.

"What's going on? Go to sleep!" shouts the Baron. "Didn't that damned traitor fall into the ravine with the truck? Take him away. We'll take care of him tomorrow"

"Take him to the Caves of Crasso!" orders Luca.

Nicola arrives and delivers a powerful punch with his right hand to Franco's face, who, unable to defend himself, tumbles and ends up between the legs of the horse.

A guard picks Franco back up and, with the other thugs, pushes him back and forth, taking turns hitting him with savage enjoyment.

Carmela, from the window, listens helplessly to the insults, mocking laughter, and curses aimed at Franco. Covering her ears, she shouts out, "Enough! You'll kill him!"

Franco, bruised and bleeding, is taken away in a jeep.

At the Caves of Crasso, inside a shack, Franco, battered and bound, is guarded by the shepherd, Battista. The door opens and Luca enters, sending away the guard. Then he approaches Franco and gives him something to drink.

To incite him, Luca tells Franco that the Baron slapped Carmela because she gave warning, and for security, he locked her up in a cellar.

"I can get her out if I please. Let's reach an accord. We are enemies who hate the same enemy, and I want to take his place," Luca tells Franco cunningly.

"Don't try to fool me. You have been at his service for years," retorts Franco.

"Let's put it this way. I free you, and you eliminate him tonight!"

Luca takes the knife with the carved wood handle out of its sheath, cuts off the ropes, and entrusts it to Franco. Then he tells him, "Hey, I want that back when you're done!"

Franco, in complicity with Luca, slips into the baronial palace. Together they free Carmela. With the help of Francesca, Carmela hides in her room to wait for events to develop.

The governess is another of the Baron's victims. For years she's been forced to serve him obediently because the Baron has been paying for her son's education.

Franco reaches Frank Cassano's study. The air is heavy with the smell of his cigar; he sees the smoke rise in the air, then the robe that protrudes from the armrests. As he nears the chair, he perceives the smell of the cologne, that fragrance that has become the sickening smell of evil.

He is now behind the armchair, ready to strike. He tightens his grip on the knife and forcefully delivers a violent blow through the back of the chair. The knife penetrates all the way from side to side, but the chair is empty. The robe spread across the chair, and the cigar burning on the ashtray, fooled him. The blade remains stuck, wedged in the back of the velvet chair.

"It didn't work out for you. You little fool!" the Baron laughs, pointing a gun at Franco.

The Baron approaches the armchair and pulls the knife, recognizing the owner.

Franco pretends first to surrender then, with a catlike jump, pulls the carpet. The Baron, standing on the other side of the mat, falls to the floor. Without hesitation, Franco plunges acrobatically through the window and lands on the pergola, which collapses and softens the blow.

The horse is ready and waiting for him. "Carmela, I am still alive! Everything is fine!" Franco shouts with all his might.

Carmela hears the message and runs to the window, but Franco is already far away.

That same night, Franco, accompanied by Michael, travels to Naples, from which point he will embark. A long and uncomfortable journey by boat awaits him, but there is no other alternative.

Someone has followed them and seen all their moves and will go back to report on them.

XV

Luca and Nicola are in the sunny square entertaining some villagers with an incredible story. "The police were coming to arrest him, and Tonio gave the alarm, shouting, "Sbrigna la contea!" Nuccio, without a second thought, jumped from the second-floor window. He says that St. Francis of Paola picked him up and placed him on the road! Since then, there are those who call him 'the miraculously saved' and those who call him 'the drunk.'"

Those present looked at each other in disbelief; they don't believe the story and leave laughing.

From the window across the square, the barrel of a lupara emerges, and behind it is the Albanian, whose aim is to shoot Luca.

He hits him with precision on the index finger of the left hand. While the man screams, the Albanian opens the window wide and shouts out, satisfied, "It hurts, doesn't it? We are even, but you will not survive because I have put curare on the bullet!"

Luca, in pain, bandages his bloody hand with a handkerchief and angrily gives Nicola a task. "Before tomorrow, bring me the head of that worm!"

"And what's in it for me?" Nicola asks.

"I will name you the heir of all that I own!" Luca responds.

That same evening, in the back of the tavern, in the bocce court, Nicola has challenged the Albanian to a game. The Albanian never refuses to play a game because he considers himself unbeatable.

"But you, Albanian, what is your name? Do you have a name?" Nicola asks.

"What do I need one for?" the Albanian replies.

"There are times when it is necessary to have a name."

Nicola is undoubtedly thinking what to write on the tomb, but luckily for him, the man is not very clever.

Nicola throws and scores to his advantage, but the Albanian, after looking him smugly in the eyes, picks up the ball and brings it to his lips, blows on it, and throws it. With a precision hit, the ball strikes and scatters the little fortress the adversary created, balls crashing against the wooden sides of the court, scattering every which way and then, slowly, as if magically, they were obeying the man's command, the balls positioning themselves in such a way as to give the Albanian the necessary points to win the game.

"You've won again! One would have to cut off your hand to make you lose!" Nicola jokes with the Albanian, who doesn't take offense to the infelicitous joke, but rather laughs about it.

They sit at the table and drink until the Albanian is drunk and staggering. Nicola is barely able to hold him up, but he manages to get the Albanian into the truck. He drives the truck until he reaches Valle Fonda, a location named because of the dense vegetation making it dark even at midday. Nicola drags the Albanian and places him with his back resting against a beech tree, then pulls out a sharp axe he had wrapped in a blanket, and savagely decapitates him. In the bedroom, precluding the wake, Luca lies feverish and delirious. At the bedside, his wife and two pious elderly women are praying the rosary. Frank Cassano, worried that the man will tell what he knows, is there to make sure that no one comes near to speak with his consigliore, a man cognizant of secrets and intrigues, least of all the priest with the pretext of hearing a confession.

The dying man, seeing Nicola come in with a cloth-covered basket, sits up, struggling, and with the last of his strength, waves to the women and sends them away.

"Wait, before I show you, I want to read the will!" Nicola reminds Luca. With sweaty hands, Luca pulls the document from under the pillow, but it is still missing the witnesses' signature.

"It is sufficient with my signature!" announces the Baron, who then signs the document and hands it to Nicola.

"It is truly a nice amount! Even too much for me!" says Nicola after reading the testament.

"You are forgetting the part you must pay me," the Baron says, laughing. "Then you'll see how much you have left!"

"Now let me see!" Luca demands in a whisper.

Nicola opens the basket, grabs the enclosed head by the hair, and shows Luca the horrific spectacle.

"You died before I did, you piece of shit!" says Luca, coughing. Then with a green face, rolling his eyes, he dies.

Nicola has cleaned up. Wearing a new suit and polished shoes, he waits for the Baron in the hall. He adjusts his tie in front of the big mirror, admiring himself like a peacock showing off its fan; he feels entitled to wander through the rooms. He reaches a room with the door ajar, where Sofia is pouring jugs of milk in a large bathtub. As he watches, the voluptuous woman undresses and gets into the tub.

Nicola enters blatantly, but Sofia doesn't seem bothered. Rather, she invites him to come forward and entices him. "It's nice! I read that in ancient Rome, Poppea would bathe herself in milk to have a softer skin. Do you want to try? Come closer…"

Nicola, aroused and confused, doesn't pay attention to the sound of the front door opening and closing. When he finally realizes what the noise was and understands the risk he is taking, he wants to run away, but the voluptuous woman retains him.

"Don't leave. Don't you find that danger makes everything more exciting? And the closer you get to it, the more stimulating it is!" Sofia steps out of the bathtub and embraces him.

Nicola cannot resist her. He gives in, and then suddenly pushes her away when he sees the Baron come in, infuriated.

The Baron shoves the woman, who falls to the floor. "This is your last betrayal, whore!"

"Don't kill me!" pleads Sofia, "I can be useful to you. Carmela is pregnant. She needs me, and I will help her!"

"She does not need your help!" The Baron vents his rage by grabbing Nicola by the neck and throwing a punch that stuns him. Then he grabs Sofia, forcefully drags her to the tub, and violently shoves the woman's head into the milk.

The woman struggles, kicks, and tries to come up for air. Bubbles emerge from the white liquid, which splashes everywhere, and then everything is quiet. The body collapses.

Nicola is shocked. The Baron breaks a bottle of salt and pushes the sharp edge against Nicola's throat.

"Don't kill me!" Nicola implores fearfully.

"Don't worry. I still need your services!" the Baron reassures him, and continues, "Get rid of the body. You know where. Afterward, you will render a great service to me. Did you hear? That shameless Carmela is pregnant. You will marry her and pretend to make amends!"

"But, does Carmela know about this?" asks Nicola.

"She will obey, and that's that!" replies the Baron harshly.

XVI

Franco, after nearly twenty days at sea, has reached his destination. He has been living with his uncle, Salvatore, for about two weeks now; he was given a room of his own, where he has placed the few things that he was able to hurriedly gather to bring along.

It is dawn. Franco wakes up startled and screams in fear, "Carmela!" Agitated and sweaty, he looks around himself confused, then realizes that it was a nightmare.

In the meantime, Zio comes in wearing pajamas, worried. "Franco, what's the matter?"

"Sorry, I hope I didn't wake up Aunt Amelia," the young man replies, panting. "It is always the same nightmare."

Zio was already up because Franco habitually wakes up very early in the morning. "Try to stay calm. It's been too short a time. You still need to get acclimated. Do you want to know how to say 'nightmare?' You say naitmar. Understand? Naitmar, okay?"

Salvatore also invites Franco to speak English with him, so that Franco can have command of the language as quickly as possible.

The air is filled with the strong aroma of coffee that Zio prepares in an old kettle, in accordance with the Italian tradition. "Let's go to the kitchen. Coffee is best when drunk boiling hot."

Franco burns his lips a bit and moves the cup away. "Uncle, your coffee is the best. It brings me back to the world like a lifesaver."

Salvatore is a cousin of Michael's and Antonio's father, so he is Franco's cousin twice removed. He is a generous man, very hospitable and obsessive about tidiness. "I love precision, which is a virtue not to be confused with nit-picking, which instead is an obsession, a disease!"

Franco cannot explain how Salvatore manages to have not a single wrinkle in his pajamas when he gets out of bed in the morning! He is chubby, moustached, and a little bold. He keeps the Calabrian traditions although he is well integrated with American ways and culture. He has two sons who have lived in New York for years. The older son is married, and, like his father, runs a restaurant; the other is a mechanic and has an office and a showroom where he sells used cars. Salvatore speaks with his wife Amelia in the Calabrian dialect so as not to forget it. He is a simple man and far from posing as a life coach, but with his way of doing things, accommodating and generous; he manages to break the resistance of even the toughest people in the end. He speaks with passiveness; he is not impulsive but takes action only after he has counted to ten. Salvatore has lived through the experience of immigrating to America.

His parents, with fear and anxiety, left Calabria with their three children, in search of work and to have a future. They were torn apart inside but in their hearts, the clod of earth that gave them birth and saw them grow up would always be alive: the wind scented with orange blossoms, the murmur of the river in their ears, the smell of the village, the warm bread, the sunrise on the Sila, the church bell at vespers. They arrived in New York after weeks of traveling aboard the ship Lombardia when Salvatore was fourteen.

Their clothes were tattered. Their luggage consisted of a pair of suitcases tied with a rope; in the luggage, they had meat left-overs, olives and dried-up bread that they had eaten during the crossing. After disembarking, they waited long hours to go through all the procedures of control of the passengers. First was the medical control where the doctors marked the sick or those suspected to be sick with chalk for further medical examinations. The next step was a rigorous procedure of document control. The immigration officer alternated between reading the documents and looking intently into the person's eyes, then interrogating, asking for identity, origin, ship name, and records. All this to eventually issue a certificate, called an inspection card, with the warning, "And make sure not to lose it!" Once out of the control area, like fish out of water, they began the search for some relative or acquaintance that had come before them, to get a foothold, referrals, advice, and information. They were like David before the American Goliath, their sling a craft, the willingness to work, some money, and a hat. Salvatore's father was a dough mixer who worked as an employee at a bakery. He opened, with much sacrifice, a small shop where he began to bake focaccia and pizzas. As the business thrived, he expanded, eventually opening an Italian restaurant that he called "La Cucina Italiana".

By the time his father retired from the job, Zio had acquired the experience and expertise to continue the restaurant. His present apartment is quite big and is located above the restaurant.

Michael, in the letter delivered by Franco, asks him to talk to a friend of his father, a fellow countryman who immigrated with Zio, someone who has come a long way and is now in a position of power; he calls himself Don Valente. He will have to tell this don what has happened to the family and the Village too long kept a Village because of the Baron.

Franco is bewildered by suddenly finding himself in a big metropolis, after coming from a small rural world and the Village life to which he was accustomed. Big streets, big buildings, big cars, giant neon signs—everything is so much bigger than what he is used to.

XVII

ON THE PATIO ADJACENT to the restaurant "La Cucina Italiana," young people are having fun and listening to music. The tables are filled with people who have come for happy hour, and there is a constant coming and going of people. Franco is wearing an ill-fitting white jacket, several sizes too big. The sleeves of the jacket are too long, covering half his hands, and get in the way of his every movement.

While Franco brings two drinks to one of the tables, he notices a Chrysler parked in front of the patio entrance and sees two individuals of despicable aspect exiting the vehicle and look around, peering curiously as though looking for someone.

Zio busily passes by the table, and Franco grabs him by the arm and starts to tell him, "Uncle, look at those two—" But the two men in question had disappeared. Zio, giving no weight to the interrupted sentence, gives Franco a reassuring pat on the back.

It's evening, and the restaurant is very crowded. Franco helps in the kitchen and, as needed, serves the tables. The two men that Franco saw earlier in the patio, Andrew and Filippio, enter the dining hall. They choose a centre table and sit down, moving the chairs noisily, and order expensive entrees and wine. The men look around jauntily and laugh with each other.

When Zio gives them the tab, they laugh in his face and refuse to pay. "If you refuse to pay, I will call the police!" Zio tells the men.

"Try calling the police, and we will break everything before they arrive!" threatens Filippio. "Rather, tell me where that Calabrian guest of yours is!"

Zio tries to buy time, hoping that Amelia will call the police. Franco comes into the dining hall from the kitchen carrying a tray with two steaming cups of coffee. He hears the men and prudently stops, which makes the cups sway on the tray.

Filippio points the gun at Zio head while Andrew holds a gun pointed at those present in the dining hall.

"Are you looking for me?" Franco interjects in rough English, smiling.

Filippio turns the weapon on the young man who now approaches the table and exchanges a quick look of understanding with Zio. "A good meal should always end with a good coffee, and Uncle Salvatore makes it extra special. It's my lifesaver!"

Together, Franco and Zio grab the cups of boiling hot coffee and throw it in the faces of the two thugs. Filippio, confused, shoots his gun, shattering the large mirror behind the counter, while with the other hand covers his burnt cheek. Zio disarms him and throws him out of the restaurant with kicks on the butt. Amelia, in the meantime, grabs the double-barrel shotgun and fires two shots to the air. Andrew, in pain, drops the weapon, and Franco pushes him all the way out of the restaurant.

"Hurray! We made them run!" shouts Franco.

"For the time being," replies Amelia worriedly. "You'll see that they'll be back. They know you're here!"

Zio is fuming. Hands on his hips, he looks at the broken mirror and exclaims, "Damn, I have to replace it immediately! And who will reimburse me for it?"

The very next day, Zio gets a shiny, new mirror installed.

The aftermath, as in an earthquake, is punctual and quick to come. It's night time and the restaurant is illuminated only by the flickering traffic lights. All of a sudden, the silence is broken by bullets shot through the wide glass windows, which shatter loudly. Glass splashes onto the tables, chairs, cabinets, and shelves that hold plates, cups, and bottles. The chandelier, studded by the numerous blows falls noisily to the floor, crashing into pieces.

Zio arrives with the double-barrel shotgun, followed by Franco with his uncle's gun. They cautiously scan the outside and respond to the fire. The shots came from the Chrysler parked in front of the store, and in the driver's seat, they recognized Filippio.

Some shots hit the neon sign, partially destroying it and making sparks everywhere. A bullet hits the new mirror and it shatters. "Damn! Again!" swears Zio, who furiously shoots like a madman to release his anger. The car takes off, skidding, does a U-turn, and disappears into the night.

After the storm, Zio takes stock of the damage, and Franco realizes the danger he is facing. "I will have to find another place to live. Staying here puts you guys in danger, as well!"

XVIII

A Few Months Later

FRANCO HAS SINCE FOUND a small apartment in a building not far from Zio. He continues to help out at the restaurant, although he continues to look for another job. In the evenings, he continues to study and refine his English, and naturally, he has come a long way; he wants to become a true American. Of course, the first words he wants to learn are swear words.

Not one day has gone by without Franco asking his uncle if a letter has come from Carmela, even though the answer is always the same. It's been a while since he last heard from Michael.

A sleek Plymouth stops in front of the restaurant. A man remains at the wheel, while another exits the car and walks toward the restaurant. Franco is always tense and on alert after what happened a few months earlier. He goes to warn Zio, but the two men did not pose any danger. They were sent by Don Bernardo to pick up Franco and Zio and take them to his office. It is on Bernardo's response to Zio's request.

Don Bernardo's office is located on the 25th floor of a skyscraper downtown.

Don Bernardo is called "The Bishop" by those who know him because he habitually goes to church every morning to help with the six-o'clock mass. The church is very close to his home, but he always goes by car, escorted by one of his loyal men.

Don Bernardo is over seventy years old, with a thin face, the gaze of an inquisitor, and a sly smile. He has a dry cough from smoking, and he dotes on his nieces and nephews. He is considered a tough guy, one who demands respect, but also a man, who respects, in his own way, all the rules, does not flaunt power and helps the needy without fanfare. He likes horses but has never ridden one. He owns a stud farm with very expensive racing horses that have often won prizes. One of his favourite pastimes is the races. It thrills him to see the horses at peak performance running toward the finish line with the impetus and momentum that distinguishes these animals. The horse-racing world is, of course, one of his most profitable businesses, and one that combines work and pleasure. He often wears his jacket resting on his shoulders, as if it were a short cape. He believes it gives him more power and authority, probably a memory from his childhood; he must have seen an uncle or someone he respected in his village carrying his jacket in this fashion.

Soon after Don Bernardo and his family migrated to America, his father, a book binder by profession, died suddenly from a heart attack; his mother, a music teacher, was not able to find a job, and Salvatore helped them in times of need by welcoming them into his home when they were hungry and did not have a place to sleep.

Later, after working for years in a factory, as Don Bernardo puts it, his luck turned. He is not very clear as to who helped him have a change of fortune, but Don Bernardo entered the field of highway construction and, soon after the contracting field, he became Don Bernardo, one who matters, one whose hand one kisses, without his being a saint.

An elderly secretary escorts Zio and Franco into Don Bernardo's office. In the smoke-filled room, Don Bernardo is sitting comfortably in the arm-chair behind the huge desk and, after a few bouts of coughing, speaks: "Zio! Long-time no see!"

"I kiss your—" Zio starts to say, but Don Bernardo interrupts, "You kiss absolutely nothing! You think that I'm senile and have forgotten the past? Unfortunately, this morning I am a bit in a hurry, so I will go straight to the point. I can't do anything for you, and it breaks my heart. Frank Cassano has many friends, and what counts most here, is that he has many businesses, and if he commits a few venial sins, well, we let him be. Of course, if he commits a mortal one, then are you Franco? Can I call you Franc?"

Franco nods shyly. Don Bernardo proceeds to tell him, "I know you are good with horses, and I love horses! I want to give you a try. But, mind you, you must not handle other people's fillies. I inquired and heard that you are a father. You have a son, and his name is Francesco. As you can see, I am interested in you."

Franco is moved by the news he has just heard, but has no time to enjoy it because he is shoved into his new job right away.

"I entrust you to Alfredo," the new boss tells Franco, and then calls out, "Alfredo, come here. This is Franc. You see to him. You know what to do."

Franco thanks Don Bernardo and leaves with Alfredo. Zio hugs Don Bernardo and leaves the office happy. Alfredo is one of Don Bernardo's trusted men. He looks tough, but his face is likeable at first sight. He is a thirty-something New Yorker and speaks pretty good Italian, though he interweaves some words in dialect because he had a friend from Bensonhurst, Brooklyn.

He started his activity with the 'ndrangheta as picciotto, then sgarrista, and later vangelista. Interrupting his career for several years while in prison, he is now a quartino, as the tattoo on the back of his hand indicates, and he is in charge of the drivers, assigning the shift and the escort vehicles to each.

Taking the private elevator, Alfredo takes Franco to the garage, a bunker, secured and monitored, where the luxury cars owned by Don Bernardo are parked, a real collection of vehicles. Don Bernardo, as a precaution, changes cars often. However, he has kept the same personal chauffeur for years. At the far end of the huge garage is the room where the drivers gather to wait for their vehicle assignments.

Alfredo and Franco get in one of the vehicles to tour the city. It is not for a tourism purpose but to give the city a once-over, to get to know the negative aspects of the city, the ones pertaining to delinquency and social malaise. It is a field trip, to give the rules and provide training to the new recruit on his new activity.

Alfredo's driving experience comes from drag racing; thus, his driving is reckless. Using a handkerchief so as not to leave any fingerprints, Alfredo takes a gun from the car's glove compartment and hands it to Franco.

"You have to watch out for spies!" Alfredo warns Franco. "There are many unsuspected and treacherous infiltrators; these men are working for the Goffredo family, of Sicilian origin, the city's most powerful enemy."

Alfredo and Franco arrive at an establishment on the outskirts of the city to pick up one of the drivers, who, due to an emergency, had to stand in for one of the night guards. The man comes out of the control booth, and another takes his place.

The man they are picking up has a gun visibly tucked into his belt. Franco recognizes him. It is Filippio! What a coincidence! It's not possible! But sometimes the world is truly small and the world of crime even smaller.

The man has a burnt, scarred cheek. Filippio acts indifferent and pretends not to recognize Franco.

"Is he a new hire you have to babysit?" Filippio asks Alfredo scornfully.

"Shut up and get in!" Alfredo replies, annoyed.

Franco remains impassive but fears for his safety. Filippio was surely commissioned to kill him and is definitely a mole, a spy, but he cannot report him to Don Bernardo's men because no one would believe his story. While in the car, Franco notices that the killer is wearing a very expensive watch and on his little finger has a diamond ring that he nervously turns around on his finger.

XIX

Franco decides to follow Filippio; he wants to find out more, even if the quest might prove dangerous. He wonders who might have commissioned Filippio to kill him and how a driver can afford such expensive jewellery. Taking all precautions, Franco shadows Filippio for the next few days but gets no answers.

Franco does not lose heart and continues his quest with caution and perseverance. He is weary; the results he was hoping for by shadowing Filippio seem unavailable. Then one night he sees Filippio cautiously entering one of the processing plants where the Goffredo family has their bovine meat import–export business.

Filippio is a spy, one of those unsuspected and treacherous moles that Alfredo was talking about. Not only is Franco's life in danger, but most likely also the life of Don Bernardo. At this point, Franco must continue his investigation, and even risk death.

One day, while Filippio is assigned to an escort job that will take up his entire day, Franco seizes the opportunity to sneak into the killer's home. Franco searches drawers, closets, and the entire apartment with no results. Then he notices some wooden crates stacked in an elevated storage area, reachable only with a ladder. Franco sees no ladder inside the apartment; in fact, Filippio has hidden it outside the window, latching it with a hook. This intrigues Franco, who manages to find the ladder and climbs up to the storage area.

In one of the crates, Franco finds a homemade time-bomb, ready to be used at any time. Searching in the garbage can for more clues, he finds a crumpled road map of the city amid the trash.

Franco opens the map on the table. He notices a circle marking the location of Don Bernardo's office, with the opera house marked with an X, and the streets leading to it clearly marked. Each path shows travel time in minutes and seconds; the bomb will detonate at the place and time established as the preset route.

The date is already set, the opening night of the opera season, a well-established tradition of Don Bernardo. Filippio has been commissioned with the task of placing the bomb under the boss's car. But how can Franco expose him in front of everyone? Franco puts everything back as he found it, leaves no trace behind, and silently walks away. However, while he is walking down the hallway, a door closes; perhaps someone from a neighbouring apartment might have seen him.

In the days that follow, Franco tries to act normal so as to not raise any suspicion. But one day, while sitting at a table having lunch, he gets a sinking feeling as Filippio comes to sit next to him. Franco has cold sweats, as he fears that Filippio suspects he has been in his apartment. Nonetheless, Franco finds the courage to talk to Filippio about sports and other banalities, to avoid questions that might incriminate him.

Alfredo is sitting two tables away from Franco. When Filippio leaves, Franco has the thought of telling Alfredo about the whole situation but changes his mind, fearing that Alfredo and Filippio might be accomplices.

Franco arrives home and tries to turn on the lights, but they don't come on. Three men are waiting for him in the dark and try to grab him. Franco, with a jump of acrobatic agility, wiggles free and, with punches and kicks, neutralizes the attack.

In the scuffle, the apartment is turned upside down. Franco jumps out the window and, landing on the roof, flees. As soon as the thugs see his silhouette running, they begin shooting, and two of them chase him, running between the chimneys and jumping from ledge to ledge.

Franco slips through a terrace door and dashes down the rickety stairs leading to the alley, but the third killer, perhaps the chief of the thugs, blocks his way. Franco cannot make out his face, as it is covered by a stocking.

While struggling with the killer, Franco feels a sharp object, sharper than a razor blade, dig into his hand. Franco manages to free himself and quickly breaks into a warehouse of bottles and barrels. The pursuers arrive, and Franco begins throwing bottles and rolling barrels toward the thugs, causing them to stumble, and opportunistically flees the scene. When Franco returns home, he notices that the glass of the window from which the killer entered was cut with precision with a diamond-tipped instrument. Franco prefers to take a risk and reveal to Alfredo what he discovered at Filippio's home, even if there is no other proof inside the crates or the markings he saw on the map of the city. Alfredo is not at all surprised by the story; apart from disliking Filippio personally, he has never really trusted the man. By word of honour, he believes Franco.

Alfredo carefully assesses the dangerous situation, as a bomb puts many lives at risk. He will come up with a plan to entrap Filippio and expose him in front of everyone.

Alfredo is in charge of organizing the entourage of vehicles that will transport Don Bernardo, his wife, and a couple more guests, to the Opera on opening night. He gathers the drivers, including Filippio, to assign them the vehicle each will be driving. "The cars will drive out in the order that I tell you. Come by the office so I can give you the written instructions," Alfredo tells the drivers.

At a pre-determined time, Don Bernardo and his guest exit the elevators into the garage. The four limousines, each of a different make and model, are lined up, each driver standing next to his assigned vehicle. The boss is about to board the Buick limousine, but Alfredo stops him. "Don Bernardo, wait!"

Franco, dressed in a suit, goes under the vehicle and removes the time-bomb. The boss shouts, infuriated, "Who checked the vehicles?"

"Franco and I," responds Alfredo. "We inspected the vehicles and found the bomb earlier; we defused it and put it back where we found it. The purpose of this charade is to unmask the spy lurking among us."

Alfredo proceeds to show Don Bernardo some papers. "I had each driver sign a paper acknowledging the vehicle assignment, but I only wrote that you would be traveling in the Buick on one of the papers, the one Filippio signed!"

With that information, Filippio is nailed. Alfredo continues, telling Don Bernardo that the prior night, Filippio, fearing he had been discovered, went to Franco's apartment and cut through the window in Franco's room with the diamond tip from his ring, with the intention of killing Franco, but that he only managed to cut Franco on his hand. To validate the accusation, Franco shows the cut on his hand to Don Bernardo.

Filippio, unmasked, flees. Having no other way of escape, runs to the bathroom. After a few seconds, knowing that he will be caught, he shoots himself.

Don Bernardo is saved, thanks to the ability of the two young men, and a bond of friendship between Franco and Alfredo is born. Alfredo has been a thug much of his life. In spite of this, he is a loyal man. He was born and raised in the social environment of crime, which formed his personality. All he knows is a life of crime. Nonetheless, he follows a code of honour. He knows and understands that his condition will never improve, that it is too late to change his way of life; he has been crippled by a higher force.

XX

Two Years Later

Don Bernardo has purchased a valuable head of cattle, a Hereford bull to breed to increase the production of meat for export. With this new acquisition, it will be easier to compete in the foreign markets against Guido Goffredo.

The agreement includes the purchase of a brown pure-bred Kentucky horse, a birthday gift he plans to give to his niece. Franco and Albert will have to go pick up the two specimens in a town up south, west of Virginia, in Lexington.

Lexington, Kentucky

Franco heads the challenging task of loading the bull onto the pickup equipped for livestock and placing the purebred in the trailer hitched to the jeep.

Two other men, along with Franco and Albert, get in the Packard, ready to retake the trip back home with the precious cargo secured. The journey of about 900 miles north will definitely be riskier and more difficult than the one going south.

The entourage travels nonstop day and night. When they get tired, they make short stops to stretch their legs and, more importantly, to refresh the precious animals.

The trip runs smoothly on the interstate, with no unforeseen obstacles. They cross New Jersey, meaning only fifty miles remain to get to New York. As they reach the southern outskirts of the city, in the rear view mirror they spot a car that already has been following them at a distance of about a mile. It is night time, driving down a straightaway, when a truck pulls out from a side road and stops in the middle of the road, blocking the way. The vehicle that was following them which has three people aboard, stops right behind them, bottling in Franco and his cohorts. Shots are fired simultaneously from the truck and the car behind them. They are trapped between the two firing squads!

The escort vehicle leaves the roadway at full speed, swerving to avoid the truck, followed by the jeep with the trailer, which bounces dangerously. However, the pickup with the bull inside doesn't quite make it and smashes into the cabin of the truck. The gunman and the truck driver are expelled from the truck, and the pickup driver dies instantly on impact.

The truck bursts into flames and there is a risk that the pickup with the bull inside will also catch on fire. The two killers shooting from the vehicle are hit, and the driver, fearing for his life, makes a U-turn and flees at full speed. As he will probably go to call reinforcements and could return within a short time, it is prudent to evacuate as quickly as possible. In the dark, illuminated by the headlights of the vehicle, Franco, along with Alfredo and the other two men, get the horse out of the trailer, and, in its place, they manage to place the bull. They make it just in time because the pickup bursts into flames and explodes as soon as they have the bull secured inside the trailer. They hitch the trailer to the Packard, and the jeep is left on the side of the highway.

"Go now, with the trailer hitched to the car. You'll get there sooner!" orders Franco.

"And how will you return?" asks Alfredo.

Franco places a blanket on the horse's back, improvises a bridle, and tells Alfredo, "I grew up among horses! I will see you in New York. Keep your eyes peeled!"

Franco will have to ride for several miles and doesn't know how long it will take him. He stops often because he doesn't want to tire the purebred that must be delivered to Don Bernardo in good shape.

He doesn't know the area but does everything possible to pass through the countryside and non-inhabited areas; he wants to avoid crossing through the city and areas with heavy traffic. He takes the back roads and goes in search of land where the horse can graze and find water to drink. Not finding any such place, he takes advantage of the parks he finds along the way throughout the city.

It is a very risky operation, for he must absolutely avoid any accidents for himself and the purebred. He must deliver it safely to its final destination; Don Bernardo doesn't tolerate mistakes.

Alfredo delivers the bull in great condition to Don Bernardo's ranch. He relates to the boss the ambush they suffered, how they resolved it, and that Franco had embarked on a journey riding the purebred. Don Bernardo, startled, considers the venture to be very risky and impatiently lights another cigarette.

Later in the afternoon of the following day Don Bernardo, riding in his limousine, exits the garage of the skyscraper and merges into traffic. Franco, on horseback, draws alongside the vehicle and beckons the driver to slow down. From the window, Don Bernardo sees the magnificent horse and instructs the driver to stop. He lowers the window and leans out.

"It's a great specimen, is it not?" exclaims Franco. "Worthy of your niece!"

Don Bernardo is astonished. At first he is a little irritated, then he lets out a smile of satisfaction, proud of the purebred which passers-by stop to admire.

"Franc, you are truly a good *picciotto!*" Don Bernardo proudly tells Franco.

Don Bernardo invites Franco to the riding school to introduce him to his niece, Maria, who will be riding the purebred. Maria is a beautiful twenty-year-old girl; she studies literature at the university. Don Bernardo has also invited her boyfriend, a fellow student, and his parents.

In front of the guests, Don Bernardo tells of Franco's prowess and the young lady admires him as a hero. Franco gives a demonstration of his special riding skills, and Maria, out of affinity, expresses her fondness and watches him, mesmerized, with a look that leaves no doubts. Franco reciprocates the look, and Don Bernardo, ever watchful, notices. "Maria, give it a name!" prompts her uncle.

"I would like Franc to choose the name!" replies Maria.

Franco is embarrassed, but he cannot refuse. Don Bernardo, very serious, fixes his gaze on him. "Go ahead, give it a nice name," urges the boss.

"I wouldn't know. Nick? Yes, Nick is a nice name," Franco answers, and all present laugh.

"Okay, I'll call it Nick!" shouts Maria. Thrilled, she kisses Franco.

Franco, embarrassed, prefers to take his leave. "Okay, I'll leave now and bid you goodbye!" He then approaches Don Bernardo. "Don't bother with the foals of others."

Don Bernardo shakes Franco's hand firmly and with the other hand encloses the handshake tightly.

XXI

Calabria

ARRANGED ON THE WALLS of the munition room of the baronial palace are a panoply of swords, spears, maces, axes, and shields of various types and eras. It is a valuable collection.

Frank Cassano, wearing a loose white shirt, is training, wielding a heavy Danish axe, holding it with both hands. Michael and Nicola watch as he trains. The don sets down the axe and goes toward a stand with throwing axes. He takes one. About ten feet from him is a wooden target resembling a human silhouette.

"Enough with the cattle crossing over to the Vecchio Mulino! Alfonso cannot send armed men to gather the scattered cows. This provocation would cost him his life!" says Frank Cassano as he throws the axe and misses the target. He takes another one, throws it, and this time hits the centre of the target.

"The francisca is a fast and deadly weapon that the Franks threw in their battles," Frank Cassano explains to those present, then changes his mood abruptly and resumes his former speech. "I order that all livestock that stray be confiscated! Alfonso wants us to go graze in his territory? Then we will set him straight with a cattle raid! Michael, go make an inspection of the land! Nicola, sharpen the axes. They're dull."

Carmela, anxious, paces in her room, wringing her hands first then bringing them to her face to cover her eyes. She checks on Francesco, who is sleeping in her room, and entrusts him to Rita, the elderly nanny. She walks down the corridor past Frank Cassano's room, stops for a moment, hesitant, looks briefly into the room, then, decided, continues on her way.

Inside the church, Carmela makes the sign of the cross with holy water and meets up with the elderly Don Benito, who is sitting in the first pew reading his breviary. She sits next to him, kneels, prays silently, then in a low voice tells the priest, "Father, I would like you to hear my confession. For years I have lived with a dark evil inside of me. I am guilty of having considered Frank Cassano my idol, fascinated by power that actually was brutality, believing in his justice that was indeed violence. I found myself without a father, and I needed a father figure, so I clung to him so as not to feel abandoned, and he took advantage of me. He often spied on my nakedness, getting too close at times. His horrible scent!"

She interrupts herself to hold back her tears, then continues, "I loved Franco, but I was tormented, not well inside my soul frozen, as if I had to always refute goodness and affection. Francesco is two years old, and Franco is so far…what will be our future? Uncle Michael handed me over to Frank Cassano without defending me. Why?"

"Probably because he chose the lesser evil," replies the understanding priest. Carmela bursts into tears. They are liberating tears.

"Ego te absolvo a peccatis tuis…" The priest whispers other incomprehensible words and concludes, "Amen." Then Don Benito holds Carmela's hands affectionately and tells her, "Go in peace."

XXII

The courtyard of Don ALfonso's baronial palace is very special and well cared for. There are many ornamental plants of various kinds, cultivated flowers, and a small botanical garden. Under the portico, Don Alfonso, with his hunting dogs, takes a stroll with Filippo.

"I've heard serious things about my brother that I hope are not true. There are also other people who are threatening to inform the central authorities. I have to stop him! Alert Cesco. We will go to the Vecchio Mulino with three men."

"Go through the valley," suggests the wise consigliore. "It is a longer route, but you will avoid passing through the Varco del Diavolo."

"Right! That damn Michael!" replies Don Alfonso.

The Location of Vecchio Mulino.

The river of Vecchio Mulino is a seething maelstrom of waves and rushing waterfalls.

Don Alfonso directs the men who, with solid metal sheets and boards, bar the waters and divert the course of the river so that the tousled waves flood the land. The water abandons the river bed and invades the farmland.

"With the fields flooded, my brother's men cannot fight against us, and it will be very easy to invade his territory!" says Don Alfonso. Then a series of shots echo in the air.

Don Alfonso, followed by his dog and the men, take cover behind the trees. "Cesco, how many are they?" asks Don Alfonso.

"I cannot see them, but they are firing from different angles. It might be five or six!" Cesco replies. The shots increase, coming from various directions.

Michael has strategically placed a series of rifles behind the beech trees and in the ravines of the hill, and now goes rapidly from one weapon to the next.

A man is hit between the eyes, and another is hit as soon as he comes out from the trees. "Don Alfonso, we've lost two ma—ah !" Cesco also falls to the ground.

"Vanni, do you see anyone?" asks Don Alfonso.

"Yes, I see Michael and it looks like he is alone!" replies Vanni.

"Let's get him in a cross-fire!" shouts Don Alfonso.

Don Alfonso reaches the construction site and climbs up the loose stairs of the building, followed by his dog. He reaches the second landing, his dog barking right behind him. He leans out to try to see Michael from on high, but Michael sees him first and fires at Don Alfonso. Luckily, the bullet only grazes him.

Vanni, perched on a dilapidated crane, manages to hit Michael on the leg but then gets hit by a bullet and falls.

The duel between the two surviving men begins; they move from one hiding place to another.

Above the landing where Alfonso is hiding is a bucket drain connected to the crane. Michael, bleeding, drags himself to the crane's control panel and pulls the lever, activating the noisy machinery and pouring the mixture of concrete and gravel onto Alfonso who, taken by surprise, fails to escape from that rain of cement while his dogs leap to safety. Alfonso, blinded and gasping for air, missteps and falls into the huge tub filled with quicklime, sinking slowly into the white sludge. Michael stops the machinery and, limping, reaches the large basin from which Don Alfonso's finger emerges with his sealing ring.

Alfonso's ring is now in the hands of Frank Cassano, who examines it while Michael approaches. He notices that Michael is hurt but minimizes the incident.

"Still a great proof of loyalty!" the Baron tells Michael. Then the Baron changes his tone and begins to study Michael from a distance, tapping his head with his index finger.

"Tic, tic, tic…There is still that bug in my head. Instead of hating me, you continue to show me loyalty."

Michael, who knows the man well, senses the danger but shows confidence.

The Baron continues, "Yet you have always denied that you helped Franco escape to America! You are a liar, and I don't forget the past! I am certain it was you who did it! You are like Luca, who wanted to take my place and so passed confidential information about my business to my brother."

The Baron walks around Michael, and Michael tries to move with him to protect his back. Moving with difficulty because of the wound in his leg, Michael is now in the wolf's trap.

The Baron grabs the knife from the fruit dish and violently slashes Michael on the cheek.

Michael utters a beastly shriek and, doubled over in pain, blocks the gush of blood with the lapel of his coat. Gathering all his strength, he tries to jump on the man, but the Baron point his revolver at him while his mastiff growls in the corner.

"You can go now, but you are banned from my territory, and I will put a price on your head. I don't want to see you ever again!" threatens the Baron.

Michael rushes to the door in pain, climbs onto the horse with much difficulty, and rides away at full gallop.

XXIII

New York

Don Alfonso was respected and esteemed as a man of honor, and with his death many relevant business transactions he had going are put on hold, perhaps never to be resumed. The death ordered by Frank Cassano is considered to be a serious offense and an inconsiderate act against the rules of honorable society; untouchables can be judged and condemned only by the chiefs gathered in assembly.

Don Bernardo presides over the meeting of the bosses sitting around the table.

"It's unforgivable!" Andrew intervenes. "The trespassing of the cattle was just an excuse! He is guilty of continued acts of violence!"

"I agree," replies Don Bernardo. "Joseph, what do you think?"

"To you, Don Bernardo, we owe obedience," says Joseph, who is originally from Calabria. "But I would like to break the lance in favor of Frank Cassano; it is true that he is responsible for violence, but those who know the land he governs as well as I know it, will agree that it is a rugged land, hard and impervious, as difficult as the people who eat its fruits, and it takes an iron fist to command there."

"But to kill a brother is something else!" interrupts Don Bernardo. "And you, Matteo, who would ship cigars to him?"

"We could give him a chance to reflect," says Matteo kindly, as he knocks the ashes from his cigar butt. "Maybe we can send him on vacation for a little while."

"He did wrong!" intervenes a decided Joseph J. "Any dispute he had with Alfonso should have been reported to the court of the feud."

Matteo quickly crushes his cigar in the ashtray, completely filled by now, stirring up dust. Don Bernardo stands in front of Matteo, picks up the cigar butt between his index finger and his thumb, and shows it to everyone. "Whoever is guilty of serious offenses must be put away forever!" Don Bernardo aspirates on the cigar butt patiently until it slowly reignites, then continues, "Otherwise he comes back, as you can see, and will again do damage! I have investigated and found that Frank Cassano is a leaf, a vile traitor, an ally of Guido Goffredo who ordered the death of Alfonso because he suspected their agreement! We must now do justice!" He puts out the cigar completely.

The bosses proceed to vote, and the decision is unanimous.

Zio receives a letter with the news that Antonio, seriously ill, is in the hospital of Cosenza. Antonio's leg was amputated due to the advance necrosis and irreversible gangrene resulting from the frostbite he suffered on his foot while at war. Franco was given the news by his uncle and would like to leave immediately to assist his father and comfort his mother, but Don Bernardo must be the one to establish the departure date.

Don Bernardo, acting on the unanimous decision taken by the bosses to end Frank Cassano's dominion, decided to send Franco to Calabria to carry out a mission. The condemned Baron has already been alienated and can no longer count on the support system that has carried him throughout the years and allowed him to commit excesses.

The boss summons Franco to give him the instructions to follow in order to lure the traitor into a trap. Franco, with his uncle's help, and without arousing suspicion, will have to monitor the Baron's every move, whom he meets with, and above all, every one of the Baron's planned activities in advance. Franco is not to take any initiative on his own but only take action when a pre-established signal is given: the phrase that Don Bernardo had him read from a piece of paper that Michael then burnt with the same match he used to light his cigarette.

Michael must be the one to eliminate the Baron. In this way he will avenge the murder of Alfonso, although he had only been following an order.

Don Bernardo can see in Franco's face that he is perplexed and fearful of the outcome of the mission, but the boss reassures him.

Franco is to land in Naples and from there to continue by train. So that no one will see him arrive, he will get off the train at a station far away from the village, where Michael will pick him up. All the other details, Franco will get from Michael before his departure. At any rate, the boss does not want Franco to remain involved with the organization. In fact, he does not consider him to be contrasto onorato, a candidate fulfilling his apprenticeship before being accepted into the honourable society.

When the mission is completed, Franco will be free of any ties to the organization. "If you want, come back here with Carmela and Francesco," says the well-wishing Don Bernardo to Franco. "Open a restaurant like Salvatore's, and if by chance we meet, don't greet me. We have never met or even seen each other. Good Luck!"

Zio takes Franco to the airport. Franco would like to ask him the meaning of the curious nickname before leaving, but does not have the courage to do so, preferring to rack his brain with abstruse explanations.

Franco's plane takes off from New York to begin his return to Calabria.

XXIV

Calabria

MICHAEL WAITS FOR FRANCO at the established place then they head to the village on horseback. Along the way, Michael tells Franco about Antonio's death. Traveling at night to take advantage of the darkness to avoid being seen, they arrive home where Laura receives Franco with a warm hug. Franco talks to his uncle late into the night. He tells him of his American adventures and gives him the specific instructions he has received.

At dawn, they go to the cemetery to visit Antonio's tomb. While Laura prays at the gravesite, Michael, with bottled-up anger and much difficulty, finds the courage to tell Franco that by order of the Baron, Carmela had to marry Nicola.

Franco's reaction is one of anger. His uncle gets him to calm down and tells him that on his deathbed, Antonio made him promise that he would kill the Baron, an act of justice after so many years of harassment and crimes. Franco is impatient and cannot resist the desire to see Carmela and the child, so he sneaks into the small building, owned by the Baron, where Carmela and the child live with Nicola. He reaches the first floor, avoids the maid, and quietly opens the door of the bedroom. He sees Carmela, who is getting dressed in front of the mirror. He approaches, making sure the woman sees his image in the mirror. Carmela's heart skips a beat. Startled but glowing, she turns around, and they hug and kiss impetuously.

Carmela has remained a beautiful slim woman, though her face, framed by long black hair, shows a few wrinkles and her gaze is somewhat sad and worn.

Franco looks intensely into her eyes.

Eyes as black as coffee, as black as coal, as black as squid ink. Eyes that have laughed and shed a river of tears of pain and pleasure. They are eyes that make you laugh and shed a river of tears of pain and pleasure, as well. Eyes that speak without uttering nonsensical words, that touch without the use of unnecessary hands; that make you speak, too, without uttering nonsensical words or touch using unnecessary hands. Eyes that call and shout; that incite and whisper. A gaze that comes from the depth of her being to enter into the depth of your being, excitement, desire, shivers, a knot in the throat.

These are Carmela's eyes.

A child about three years of age enters the bedroom rambunctiously. Franco, spellbound, approaches him and asks Carmela, "Is he…?"

"Francesco, my big man!" replies Carmela.

Franco gasps. He kneels down in front of the little one and hugs him tight, almost suffocating him with affection. Carmela joins in. They move to the living room.

"I learned today of the atrocity the Baron has committed! You could have written me," Franco tells Carmela.

"I found out that he was blocking and destroying all the letters I mailed to you," Carmela replies then adds, "What do we do now?"

"Don't worry. I can't tell you yet, but I've already arranged it all," Franco assures her.

Carmela caresses him with ancient ardor, her hands tightly clutching his back with passion, as Nicola enters the room.

"Look, look who is back!" chuckles Nicola. "The American! What are you doing in my house? Get lost. There is nothing here that belongs to you!"

"Do you think I will leave and let you live in peace with my woman and my son?" retorts Franco.

"Carmela is mine. I married her, and she has long since forgotten you! She has everything. Money. Servants. I meet her every need… in every sense," replies Nicola.

Franco grabs him by the throat and nails him against the armoire. "Liar! Tell him that you are impotent!" Carmela screams furiously. "Frank Cassano used you! You even wanted me to have an abortion because you have always been jealous of Franco!"

Nicola frees himself from Franco's grip. Panting, he approaches Carmela and slaps her. The woman staggers, and Francesco runs to her in terror, screaming like a banshee.

Franco punches Nicola, who ends up on the table then falls, dragging all the trinkets with him.

Carmela tries to intervene, but she is thrown onto the maid who has entered the room. Together, they hit the glass cabinet filled with weapons, which breaks. One of the rifles slides down.

Nicola manages to grab the weapon, aims it, and shoots while Franco lunges to protect Carmela and Francesco. Franco throws a stool at Nicola and manages to disarm the man, who seems to have gone mad, raving, seemingly unable to accept the loss of the made-up family he has become accustomed to. Screaming like a madman, Nicola runs out of the room.

Franco, fearing the intervention of the Baron, and unwilling to hasten the situation, kisses Carmela and the child and cautiously leaves the house.

At the Varco del Diavolo, in front of the house, Michael and Franco are sitting on a bench. Franco cannot find peace. He finds it absurd and intolerable that his wife and son share a home with that ugly-faced Nicola. Franco is the victim of a series of adverse circumstances. When Carmela was pregnant, he had to flee; when Francesco was born, he was on the other side of the ocean; and now that he is able to embrace her, he sees his family in the hands of a stranger just because the Baron decided that it be so.

Michael reminds Franco to be patient and commit no more indiscretions now that they are so close to the day of reckoning. Franco agrees but points out that so many people are no longer present: Carmela's parents, Avellina, Gervaso, Antoinette, and Mario. Michael, to defuse the somber situation, changes the subject:

"So, in all that time, you never asked him why we call him Zio?"

"I did not have the courage, but you can tell me," says Franco.

"One of these days, I'll tell you!" Michael replies.

Franco has changed since he left; he is more mature, more of a man. Could it have been from Uncle Salvatore's tutelage? Most likely, but also from the school of hard knocks, being in direct contact with crime, where you risk being killed and must defend yourself.

The big cities should reassure you and offer protection. Instead, during dangerous encounters, the streets suddenly become deserted, as when you encounter a pack of wolves on an isolated and snow-filled plateau.

XXV

The Baron is hosting a party at the palace, in honor of Guido Goffredo, who has come from America especially to sign a contract for a very important deal. Franco, informed by Carmela, rushes to tell Michael. They will have to get into the palace to control the situation. The Baron is busy trying to convince Carmela, who doesn't want to attend the party. To not make matters worse, Carmela is pretending that she doesn't know of Franco's return.

"How can get it through to you," demands the Baron, "that this is a very important deal that will bring us major economic benefits? Plus, I have a surprise for you! Wear the red dress that is meant for special occasions. So, will you be there?"

Carmela fractiously confirms, "I'll be there…I'll be there."

Frank Cassano takes her by the shoulders and pulls her toward him to kiss her, but the woman lowers her head so that he kisses her on the forehead. The man, annoyed, hurries down the stairs and looks for a cigar, but the leather case is empty. The Baron runs into Nicola, who is coming up the stairs. "Call New York and find out about the shipment of cigars. Ask them why they have not sent them! Watch out for infiltrators, and be careful," the Baron warns Nicola, pointing at him with his index finger. "This time, I will not tolerate any mistakes!"

Nicola pulls out the revolver and humorously salutes, military style, bringing the gun barrel to the side of his forehead. From a distance, the sound of malarruni is heard. The Baron stops to think what it might mean, then dismisses it and continues on his way.

Outside the palace, men in charge of surveillance and control are placed at strategic points. Luxury cars arrive, from which elegant guests emerge. A musical group is stationed next to the buffet table, while the waiters pass among the guests with trays of shots of liquor. There are introductions, greetings, handshakes, and compliments. Groups of people stand in the hall, conversing, while others entertain themselves in the living room. The Baron diplomatically mingles with the guests, but controls the situation by giving his men strict and expressive glances, reminding them to stay alert. Franco and Michael, inside the little desecrated church near the charnel, examine a map under the light of a candle; they move the old furniture covered in dust and cobwebs, mice crawling between the feet. They pickaxe the ground to raise a huge and thick marble slab recessed into the floor, revealing steep and uneven steps that are the only way to go into the tunnel that leads to the basement of the baronial palace. They travel down the smelly tunnel, through the stream of waste drainage, ultimately finding them in front of a massive iron door, which they begin to batter down.

Franco and Michael are underground, and the loud noises from the blows to the door reverberate through the tunnel but are not heard from the upper floors. With blows from a hammer, they manage to unhinge the door and sneak into the basement of the palace. They travel down the hall with caution, and up the service stairs that bring them to the first-floor hallway, from which they monitor the living room.

Guido Goffredo, accompanied by his wife, Victoria, enters the living room, followed by a lawyer and escorted by bodyguards. Frank Cassano goes to greet Goffredo, embraces him, then introduces him to his lawyer, who has come from Naples for the occasion. Carmela entrusts Francesco to the nanny and tells her to lock the door behind her once she leaves, and to open the door to no one but her. Carmela, wearing an elegant red dress, draws the attention of those present as she descends the staircase. The Baron proudly joins her to introduce her to his guest of honor and his wife.

After exchanging compliments, the two bosses retire to the study, followed by their respective lawyers. In the meantime, the party continues in the living room with the buffet, music and dancing. After about an hour, the Baron and Guido Goffredo exit the study, pleased, while their lawyers excuse themselves and leave the palace with signed documents in their bags. In the living room, the two bosses toast their common business while the bass opera singer sings the piece "O thou, Palermo" from "The Sicilian Vespers" by Verdi, in honor of the guest, who is originally from Palermo. After the song, the Baron signals the orchestra for a waltz and opens the official dancing, inviting Carmela to the center of the dance hall.

Franco can barely hold himself back.

Unconsciously, Michael runs his hand over the scar on his cheek as he watches the Baron dancing merrily with Carmela, who appears grim and annoyed.

The Baron whispers something in her ear, appearing to be more and more euphoric as he draws closer to her. Carmela, disgusted, tries to push him away, but the man will not let go and forcefully presses against her.

Carmela reaches the boiling point when she sees Nicola guffaw and share a drink with a peasant girl. Frank Cassano notices, too, and dances her away from that squalid spectacle.

"You look beautiful in this dress," says the Baron, admiringly, "but I cannot explain why I waited so long. I have a surprise for you. I have decided to marry you, Baroness! The time has come to eliminate Nicola. His wine is poisoned!"

Carmela, furious, wriggles free and runs away. In her hurry, she gives Nicola a violent push that makes him drop his wine glass, which shatters, spilling the wine on the dress of another woman, who screams in shock.

A dark Mercedes with five men aboard stops at the gate of the palace. The guards are alerted and take action. The driver of the vehicle gives the guard at the gate a letter for the Baron and awaits a response.

The Baron, after reading the letter, authorizes the person to come in. The elegant guest has a gift package, which one of the guards unwraps and inspects carefully. It is a wooden box inside of which stands a fine bottle of champagne. The Baron lifts it as a trophy and shows it to his guests. "It comes from America!" he shouts with pride and satisfaction. The enthusiastic guests applaud.

Mister Goffredo is surprised. He is suspicious and, as a precaution, asks one of his bodyguards to take his wife, Victoria, away from the palace.

While Franco draws his gun on the balcony, he sees Carmela distraught, disheveled, and with her dress rumpled, coming out of her room with a revolver.

"Damn it! She will ruin everything," says Franco.

"I'll stop her!" suggests Michael.

"No, wait…" Franco replies.

"Quiet, please!" Shouts the Baron. "There is also a letter…" Carmela proceeds with a firm step.

The Baron unscrolls the text quickly, then turns serious, as though he doesn't understand the meaning. Nonetheless, given the circumstance, he reacts with a forced laugh.

Carmela, determined, hurries her steps, pointing her weapon in the direction of the Baron, but her hand begins to shake from excitement.

"It is a humorous phrase. I'll read it. 'Enjoy the…"

"Soperry of 45…," Franco whispers to himself.

"Say it! Say it!"

"Soperry of 45!" says the Baron, confused.

"It's the signal!" shouts Franco, as a bullet blows up the bottle the Baron holds in his hands. The Baron, puzzled and frightened, with his clothes soaked in champagne, takes cover.

The shot was fired by Alfredo with a precision rifle.

Carmela stops and wants to return to her room, but the scrambling of people prevents her, and she hides behind furniture. Franco sees Alfredo and his men. He is surprised by the unexpected arrival, but certain that it was planned by Don Bernardo.

The bloody shootout continues between the men of the Baron, Mr. Goffredo's bodyguards, and Alfredo's gang.

Franco engages in a furious battle with Nicola, but one of the Baron's bodyguards runs to Nicola's aid, and Franco is knocked out while the scoundrel escapes. Carmela sees Nicola fleeing and chases after him. When she reaches him, she pushes him to the ground. "Wait, I will do whatever you want!" pleads Nicola, sweating and shaking. "I'll eliminate Frank Cassano so that you will inherit everything!"

Carmela burst out in a hysterical and angry laugh, and lowers the weapon. "You are done hurting me!" She lifts her arm to shoot him, but Alfredo, from a distance, centers his aim right on Nicola' forehead. The rifle fires, and Carmela lets her arms down alongside her body, exhausted, and drops the pistol.

The uproar continues; fist fights, screams, destroyed furniture, and broken bottles. Franco recovers and goes in search of Frank Cassano while Alfredo hunts down Mr. Goffredo. The Baron, taking advantage of the confusion, rushes into the study and grabs bundles of bank notes and documents from the safe, stuffing them into a large leather bag. Goffredo, rowdy and armed, bursts into the room.

"Help me escape," begs the Baron, desperate. "I'll give you half of my goods. Then we will return to make a clean sweep!"

Goffredo and the Baron are about to escape, but Franco and Alfredo spot them from the French doors. Goffredo shoots and misses. Alfredo returns the fire and kills him.

The Baron takes advantage of the confusion once again and runs toward the hall of arms to take shelter. Franco chases after him.

Michael catches up with Carmela, who is upset and petrified.

"Zione! Help me. Frank Cassano wants to marry me! Promise me that you will stop him!" cries Carmela to Michael.

Michael holds her affectionately. "I promise! But where is your son?" he asks her.

"He is in a safe place," responds Carmela.

Franco uses a chair to defend himself from the Baron, armed with a sword, and from his growling mastiff.

The Baron breaks the chair into pieces with strong blows from the sword and sends the dog after Franco. Franco runs to extract a francisca stuck in a wooden column. The Baron, fearing that Franco will throw it at him, turns around to retreat but trips and falls, losing his weapon.

While the Baron is on the floor, Franco forces the mastiff out of the door, then pounces on the Baron with a feline jump and is about to strike him, but hesitates, recalling the order he received from Don Bernardo.

Drops of sweat from soaked brows fall into his eyes, blurring and marring his vision.

"Don't do it! I will make you rich, very rich!" pleads the Baron. Michael, Carmela, Alfredo, and his men, burst into the room. "Stop! Don't taint yourself with him," shouts Michael. "Leave him to me."

Franco reads in his uncle's eyes the uncontrollable urge to take revenge and vent the hatred that has accumulated for years. It is the same desire he reads in Carmela's gaze as she tells him to back off with a nod of the head. Franco angrily throws the lance. It sticks fast in a wooden coat of arms on the wall.

The Baron runs to grab an iron mace, but Michael stops him. "No, this time we do it my way!" Michael says as he throws a knife that lodges, vibrating into the table next to the Baron.

"Duel Rusticana! You know the rules! Bring it on, Baron!" challenges Michael.

Michael rolls his jacket around his left arm and opens the knife.

Frank Cassano also prepares himself.

The duelists study each other, circling around in a macabre dance, as is the custom. The gory challenge to the death begins. There are approaches, steps, missed strikes, jumps, shoves, thrusts, cuts, and wounds.

During the melee, Michael whispers into the ear of the Baron, "I have to follow the order that comes from New York. Don Bernardo and the others have condemned you to death!"

"I don't believe it. I still have friends who count!" says the Baron, who disengages, jumps back, and threatens Michael with a small two-shot pistol. "It is Carmela's, a gift for self defense. She was nervous, and I took it while we were dancing. I have decided to marry her. She is bound to me by a deep and perverse feeling of hatred and love. She saw the power in me with the eyes of a child, and now with the passion of a woman. I desired her from the moment I snatched her from your hands. She is clever and knows which side to choose. She has had good schooling!" Michael blazes with rage and jealousy. Franco trembles.

"All weapons on the floor or I'll kill him!" shouts the Baron.

Alfredo signals his men, who immediately lay down their guns.

"Carmela, take a gun and come here. Let's take Michael hostage and leave undisturbed. I will be back with my Sicilian friends, and we will put everything back in its proper place," says the Baron.

Carmela doesn't move.

"I order you to come here!" The Baron threatens. "I'm not joking. I'll shoot him and then Franco!"

The Baron proves his intention by lifting the hammer and pulling the trigger, but the gun is not loaded.

"I've never had it loaded!" Carmela says mockingly. "I would have shot you every time you've come near me, you worm!"

The Baron, dumbfounded, did not expect that attitude. Michael quickly gets the Danish axe from the panoply and spins it in the air with both hands. "Remember that worm in your head? You always wondered why, in spite of your wickedness, I have always stayed close to you? Here is the answer! Carmela don't look!" With determination, Michael hits the Baron across the neck, cutting off his head with one blow.

Carmela covers her eyes with her hands. Franco and the others present are disgusted by the gruesome scene. Carmela, in tears, hugs Franco while Michael tosses the bloody axe to the side. Alfredo leaves, followed by his men, while Don Benito comes into the hall to bless the corpse.

The survivors, confused and frightened, scatter from of the palace. The people crowd into the square as the sacristan rings the bells. The villagers form little groups, and the news of the death of the tyrant travels from mouth to mouth and becomes the subject of comments, opinions and discussions:

"After years of violence, at last he's paid for it!"

"Where was the State until now?" "It was self-defense."

"He was also a child of God!"

"And what about the children of God he killed?"

"When you kill the wolf that killed all the sheep, everyone says, 'Poor wolf!' Nobody says, 'Poor sheep!'"

"I remember when, in his arrogance, he brought Carmela to the palace. She was a little girl!"

"An act of justice! If the State wouldn't do it, someone had to do it!"

Franco and Michael, shaken up, walk out of the door of the palace, and many Villagers come up to hug them, make a comment, and shake their hands.

Michael could run away and hide like a bandit, go into hiding like a robber to avoid being arrested and tried, but decides to stay and face reality, assuming responsibility for what he did and respecting the law.

Alfredo reaches Franco to shake his hand, He says, "I will tell Don Bernardo that everything went according to plan. Goodbye!"

One of the men was wounded on the hand, and Franco wants to take him to the clinic. "Better not," Alfredo replies, smiling.

Alfredo and his men get into the Mercedes and disappear into the night as if they were never there.

The Mayor excitedly gets to the square, and the truck with the Marshall and his agents arrives. Together, they do a quick inspection to gather the facts and take control of the situation.

Carmela, holding her child wrapped in a blanket, joins Franco and his uncle.

Two agents make their way through the crowd with the Marshall and stand in front of Michael. "You are under arrest. Come with us!"

"It's an injustice!" says a Villager, speaking for the whole group of people.

"The judge will decide that," replied the Marshall.

Michael, resigned to his fate, clears things up with Franco and Carmela. "I have killed a man, and I don't want to elude justice. Otherwise, I would be just like the tyrant I have just eliminated.

Calm Laura down and take care of Francesco," he tells them.

"We love you, Zione," they reply.

"Send me a letter once in a while," says Michael.

Michael gets into the police truck that has slowly made its way through the crowd.

Francesco, in his mother's arms, obliviously waves goodbye with his little hand. Carmela holds him tight and, together with Franco, leaves the square.

Franco, Carmela and Francesco take their belongings and leave for America to start a new life in the new world. They settle in New York, where they will open an Italian restaurant. They will have other children and will then be joined by other relatives. The misfortunes of the past will remain just a memory. Away from their homeland, they will never forget their roots: the harsh territory, rough and wild, that for centuries has dripped sweat and blood. In their eyes, it will always be a wonderful and extraordinary place of magnificence…their beloved land of Calabria.

www.ingramcontent.com/pod-product-compliance
Lightning Source LLC
LaVergne TN
LVHW020424080526
838202LV00055B/5033